STICKY SNARE

PAUL GALLAGHER

Caleb.

I hope you enjoy.

Best wishes,

Sticky Snare
Copyright © 2021 by Paul R. Gallagher

Second paperback edition February 2021, May 2021

ISBN 979-8-7119-8215-9 (paperback)

Dedication

This book series is dedicated to my children, Josalyne, Calestyane, Jacen, and Samara. They mean the world to me. To my wife, who has endured my constant need to write and allow me the time to do so. She is the main reason I continue to write. She had asked me once, "Why are you writing so much if you don't intend to publish it?" So, I started self-publishing my work. To my aunt Melanie, who has read this book twice and advised on grammatical corrections and pacing of the story. Without her words of wisdom, I don't think the story would have turned out as well as it did.

To my mom, who read the rough story and constantly nagged me about George and Hillary's mother. I guess, as a mom herself, she needed to know why a mom would abandon her children. To my dad, who wanted to be a writer. I can't imagine what ideas he has stewed in his mind. (Sometimes, I'm scared to ask.) He allowed me, as a child, to write on the first word processor he owned. I wrote a story called Quinsor, a fantasy that I hope to finish someday.

Chapter One
The Funeral

Hillary gazed past the translucent reflection of her nine-year-old face, looking deep into the blurring trees. She sat in the back seat of her dad's truck along with her brother, George. Her nanny, Mrs. Winstock, sat in the passenger seat and her dad, Sam, drove. They were heading to her grandmother's funeral to say their final goodbyes, something she did not want to do.

Imagining her Nana with no life saddened Hillary because she had been so full of life. According to her dad, Nana had gone to a better place, but Hillary couldn't imagine a better place than where she lived. There were fairies in the backyard to find along with George and Hillary. What place could be better?

She felt a tap on her shoulder. "What d-do you want, George?" she asked with a slight stutter.

She hadn't always stuttered. This speech impediment developed after her mother went missing a year ago. According to all the adults, the stutter should work itself out when she became older and knew how to deal with the loss of her mother.

"How are you doing?" George asked in a somber tone, fiddling with his bright red tie around his neck.

1

She didn't answer him. Instead, she drifted to the day they found out their mother went missing.

****

George and she were sitting in their foldable lawn chairs on the concrete porch. They both watched their dad make slow, methodical turns on the riding lawnmower, cutting the grass. He had cut lines of grass between the house and the rock wall, further on the other side of the property. The smell from the freshly cut grass seemed to energize her.

Along with the smell of the freshly cut grass was that of rain in the distance. Thunder echoed over the whirring sound of the lawnmower. As they watched their dad drive the mechanical beast into the shed, a police car slowly drove up the driveway, parking behind his truck.

"What are they doing here?" George asked, jumping to his feet.

"Shhh," she said, putting her finger to her lips. "I don't know, but I bet we can hear them."

They listened, and Hillary wished that she hadn't done so. Maybe if she hadn't heard the subject of the conversation, then maybe it wouldn't be true. Maybe her mother would not have gone missing. Maybe, just maybe, her mother would have driven up in place of the police car and given them all big hugs.

Two policemen in blue uniforms somberly exited the old police cruiser. The driver, a fat man with a bushy mustache, wore a large cowboy hat. The skinny passenger wore bigger clothes than he should have. They each walked to their father who had walked out of the shed.

"Is your wife here?" the fat cop asked.

"No," her dad answered. "She's in town. I think she's getting groceries. What can I do for you?"

"I'm sorry to be the bearer of bad news, Sam," the fat one said. "We spotted your wife's car on the side of the road. On the other side of the woods there." He pointed to the woods beyond the rock wall. "We were hoping that she made her way through the woods and came home."

"What do you mean?" her dad asked, putting his work gloves in his back pocket.

The skinny policeman stepped forward. "As far as we can tell, she ran off the road. She might have been avoiding an animal."

The fat cop looked down at his hat remorsefully. He uneasily turned it over in each hand. "Look, Sam, we have to ask. Does she have enemies, or could she have been running away from someone?"

"Why would she be running away from someone?" her dad asked, rather rudely.

"Her car was still runnin' when we arrived on the scene," the fat one continued. "We looked around it and in the woods, but we couldn't find any sign of her or anyone else."

The skinny one continued. "Her footprints vanished as we got into the tree line. It seems like she just walked into the woods and disappeared."

"I need to go," her dad said in an anguished voice, looking in George and Hillary's direction.

"Yes, sir," the fat one said, looking up to the sky. "I can respect that, but we have a team of people out there right now searching in the woods. The weather doesn't seem like it's gonna hold up much longer, so please stay put and wait for your wife here. If she did walk through the woods, she should show up shortly. We are gonna do some investigating in the area, to see if there was any foul play."

"Foul play?" her dad asked in shock. "Is there blood?"

"No, sir," the skinny one said quickly. He seemed to be glaring at his partner. "Not that we can find. We'll call you with any information we get. We're gonna tow the car into town; it has a flat tire. We'll get that fixed up for ya'."

"I appreciate it, officers," Sam had said, walking away from the cops. Hillary remembered seeing the worried look on her dad's face.

Her father started making phone calls to her mother's cell phone which only rang on the other end until it finally went to voicemail. At first, her dad calmly left messages. After a few hours though, he had started yelling into the phone from anger and fear.

Their Nana and Mrs. Winstock had picked the worse day to go out of town to shop and could not get back until the next day. She overheard her grandmother tell Sam that their mother would show up. That had been the only lie she ever heard her grandmother tell.

Hillary cried herself to sleep that night, not knowing how this would turn out. When she woke in the morning her stuttering had started. She did not like her new speech impediment and tried to stop talking after realizing she could not control it.

****

"Are you okay?" George asked, bringing Hillary out of her memory.

"Leave m-me alone, George," she said, turning her head back to the blurry trees. "I d-don't want to talk about it."

"Not now, George," his father said from the driver's seat, looking into the rearview mirror at him. "She is taking this very hard, like all of us."

"I would have to agree, George," Mrs. Winstock said, turning around in the passenger seat. She looked out at them through her large glasses that increased the size of her eyes by three. For a tall, old woman, she never looked frail. There seemed to be a radiance surrounding her at all times. Nobody knew her true age and she didn't show the age everyone believed her to be. "She had been a dear friend of mine and I am taking this very hard. Everyone reacts to something like this differently. For you two, I am sure it is much more difficult."

"I'm fine," George said bravely. "I'm sad and happy at the same time."

"Happy?" Hillary asked, turning her head quickly to him with a disgusted look on her face. "H-how can you b-be happy? Nana is d-dead."

"Yes," he said pointedly. "That makes me sad. But, what makes me happy is that she is finally with Papa."

The look of outrage slowly vanished from Hillary's face. "Yeah, I g-guess you're right about th-that, even th-though I don't remember h-him."

"How much further, dad?" George asked, messing with his tie. "This tie is really starting to bother my neck."

"We're here," Sam said, turning the wheel into the parking lot.

They were at the funeral home where many people had gathered outside of the doors. They all talked to one another, possibly trading stories about their Nanna. Both George and Hillary looked at each other and then at the number of people waiting to see their grandmother off.

"Wow," George said in a surprised voice. "I didn't know there were going to be so many people here."

Sam put the truck in park and turned in his seat to look at his children. "All of these people were Nana's clients. She and Papa had the business for many years, which I now handle; taking care of these folk's lawns."

"That's w-what you do n-now, r-right?" Hillary asked.

"Yeah," he answered. "I took over their business after Papa passed away. Now listen, you two stay with Mrs. Winstock when we get inside. After the funeral, she will drive you to the cemetery."

"Where are you g-going to be?" Hillary asked.

"I am a pallbearer," Sam answered. "I will be helping move Nana from the funeral home to the hearse and then to the cemetery."

Mrs. Winstock unbuckled her seatbelt hastily. "What is he doing here? He shouldn't be here."

"Who?" Sam asked, turning away from them. He looked around in an attempt to find someone in the crowd who should not be attending his mother's funeral.

"That, Mr. Drake," Mrs. Winstock scowled, opening her door.

"Him?" Sam asked quizzically. "I invited him."

Mrs. Winstock stopped halfway out of the door and turned to him. "Why would you invite that low life to your mother's funeral?"

"That's a bit harsh," Sam said. "My mom didn't like that man because of his ceaseless nagging about buying that acreage behind the house. I hardly see that as a reason to ban the man from paying his respects."

"Pay his respects?" Mrs. Winstock said angrily. "He is not here to just pay his respects. He is a slimy snake who is up to no good."

Sam cleared his throat and hitched a thumb to the two children sitting in the back seat, staring intently at the two of them.

Mrs. Winstock put on a smile of credulity and nodded her head at them. "Please excuse me, children. I am going to go have a pleasant chat with Mr. Drake." She shut the door and walked off toward an elderly, baldheaded, hefty man standing alone on the sidewalk.

George and Hillary both got up and rested their heads on the back of the front seat. They watched Mrs. Winstock intently as she reached the man. As soon Mrs. Winstock reached the man, she pointed a finger at him and then looked back to the truck as if she could feel their little eyes upon her. She dropped her finger but continued to talk. Mr. Drake held a smile on his face for the entirety of the one-sided conversation, not removing his gloved hands from their resting spot atop of his long, slender, black cane.

"He sort of looks like a snake, dad," George said, noticing the way his lips vanished as he smiled. It looked creepy.

"I hate s-snakes," Hillary said, shaking her body as if she had the chills. "I really d-don't like f-fat snakes."

"Hillary, you don't say things like that," Sam reprimanded her.

"Sorry, d-dad," Hillary shamefully said.

"Okay, kids," Sam said. "We have to get into the funeral home."

Mrs. Winstock finished talking to Mr. Drake and she walked to the funeral home's double doors, waiting for the rest of the family. Instead of following Mrs. Winstock, Mr. Drake looked at the truck and bowed his head slightly, then walked away from the crowd.

Inside, Mrs. Winstock sat next to George and Hillary with her hands resting peacefully on her lap. People stood up and talked for what seemed like forever about how Mrs. Lana, their

Nana, had always helped them through some crisis with their yard. Many people talked of her kindness, her generosity, and her big heart. 'Her soothing voice,' an elderly man mentioned at one point. 'The biggest green thumb anyone had ever seen,' some lady said. Hillary had snickered about that statement, earning her a jab in the side from George. She tried whispering to him how she had never seen a green thumb on her grandmother, but only got an ugly look in return.

As the funeral ended, people stood up from the pews and walked up to say their last goodbyes. George and Hillary both deferred from seeing their Nana's peaceful body on view for the world to see.

The line finally came to an end and everyone left the funeral home. Sam, and five other men the children did not know, slowly carried the casket of their Nana to the hearse without saying a word. The still silence seemed clamorous.

Hillary, George, and Mrs. Winstock got into the truck, preparing for the short drive to the cemetery. Hillary observed how it didn't look right for Mrs. Winstock to be in the driver's seat. She seemed so tiny behind the wheel of the big vehicle. "Put your seat belts on, children."

As George buckled his seat belt, he asked, "Why did you not want that man-," George started to ask before Hillary corrected him.

"Mr. Drake, the s-slimy s-snake," she said smiling as if proud of herself.

George glared at her. "Why did you not want him at the funeral?"

"Your grandmother didn't like him," she said.

"But-," George tried to ask.

"No more questions about him," Mrs. Winstock cut him off while starting the truck. Mrs. Winstock drove the truck out of the parking lot carefully. "We have more important things to take care of on this solemn day."

And there were no more questions about Mr. Drake, as bad as he wanted to ask. He wanted to know why Mrs. Winstock didn't want him at the funeral. Could the man be that bad of a person to be denied to see his grandmother off? For his Nana not to like him, he must be very bad, because Nana liked everyone. He did know that he didn't like the man's slimy smile.

At the cemetery, there seemed to be many more people. The children looked around as they walked to a green tent set up in front of the casket. A mound of excavated dirt had been set off to the side of the tent. Green carpet covered the hole below the casket and the mechanism designed to lower it into Nana's final resting spot. Metal chairs, covered in green rug-like cloth with the name 'Piccadilly's Funeral' embroidered on them, were aligned for the many people attending the graveside services.

Sam stood at the front of the chairs, waiting for his family. They all sat down, George to the right of Sam and Hillary to the left. Hillary held Mrs. Winstock's hand, enjoying the warmth her hands gave off.

As the preacher said a prayer, Hillary looked at her father and watched a single tear leave his eye and travel down his cheek. She reached up, wiped it away from his face, and gave him a big hug. "I am s-sorry d-daddy."

"Me too," he said, smiling slightly.

The service ended and everyone mingled around the flower-covered casket, talking amongst themselves. George heard many stories of his Nana saving a tree on its death bed; or how the flowers in a bed had been raised from the dead in a matter of a day.

Hillary wandered off by herself and leaned against a tree, staring at the casket. She smiled at the thought of her Nana opening the lid, sneaking away before anybody could see her. She had been a wonderful grandmother.

Hillary remembered the times her Nana would comfort her when thoughts of her mother crept up on her. Nana held her tight and would caress her hair. "Don't worry, Hillary," she would say. "Someday, you will be with her again."

Tears welled up and she quickly wiped them away, not wanting to feel the tears creep slowly down her face. "I am g-going to miss you, N-Nana."

"Me too," George said beside her.

Hillary became ridged and then turned her face from George, afraid for her brother to see her cry. "W-Why are y-you sn-sneaking up on me?"

"I'm just checking on you," he said.

"I'm not a b-baby," she said, folding her arms in front of her.

"No one said you were," he responded. "I felt that I needed to check on you. I miss her and I know you do too."

"Yeah," Hillary said, relaxing. "She helped us when d-dad couldn't. You know, when m-mom left us. I loved her f-for that. She understood the way we f-felt. She never became angry when I cried at n-night. She held m-me."

"She helped me too," George said, putting an arm around his little sister.

They watched everyone disperse from the site and walk to their cars. Their grandmother's casket lay in the open, alone. Hillary couldn't believe that her Nana lay in there.

A movement in the air caught her attention behind the casket. A large swarm of bees had flown from the woods to her Nana's casket.

"Do you see that?" George asked Hillary.

"Yeah," she responded. "They are pr-probably attracted by the fl-flowers."

"Not that many," he said. "That's weird."

The bees landed on the casket, covering the majority of the lid. As the bees shifted back and forth, the sunlight seemed to reflect off their wings, creating a rippling effect. This effect reminded George of dark water rippling towards the shore of a lake they had once visited a few years back. Hillary stepped toward them and George grabbed her shoulder.

"Don't," he said. "If we bother them, they could attack."

They both watched confusedly as a glimmering light appeared in the center of the bees. The bees flew from the casket, gathered back in a swarm, and flew off into the trees. They disappeared just as quickly as they had appeared.

"Why did they do that?" Hillary asked.

"I don't know," George answered, not sure what to make of the experience. "Did you see that light, Hillary?"

Hillary, unable to wrap her young mind around what she had just seen, nodded her head. "I saw it."

Chapter Two
The Book of Fairies

Hillary and George ran from their Nana's graveside after witnessing the unimaginable sight of the bees carrying a light from their Nana's casket. George's red tie flapped behind him like a flag as Hillary trailed behind him in an attempt to keep pace.

"Dad!" George yelled excitedly when he saw Mrs. Winstock and his dad. He came to an abrupt stop in front of the two, placing both hands on his knees while gasping for air.

Sam and Mrs. Winstock abruptly ceased their conversation so Sam could kneel beside George. Sam being concerned for his son, placed a hand on his son's shoulder. "Are you okay?"

"Yes," George said, out of breath.

Hillary finally reached them and she copied her brother, leaning over and grasping her knees. "We…saw…bees."

"What?" Sam asked, not sure why the kids would be so excited over bees.

George stood, taking one last deep breath. "There…were…bees. A lot…of bees."

Sam laughed at this. "You didn't get stung, did you?"

"No," Hillary said. "Th-they w-were on t-top of Nana's box."

George made a large half-circle with both arms in the air over his head. "There were this many, or maybe more."

Mrs. Winstock patted the boy's head. She giggled the words, "Now, that's a lot of bees."

"They h-had a l-," Hillary said.

"Light," George quickly interrupted her. "A small, bright light glowed in the center of them."

Hillary glared at her brother. She didn't like it when he interrupted her because she felt dumb as if her stuttering inconvenienced him.

Sam stood, shaking his head. "A light?"

His question, George felt, had been a little on the disbelieving side.

"Yes," George said. "I know it doesn't make sense. They landed on the box and then a light appeared; a small, bright light. Then the bees all left, with the light in the middle of them."

"Are you sure a light came from your Nana's casket?" Mrs. Winstock asked, furrowing her eyebrow while lowering her head to him.

"I d-don't know it c-came from the c-casket," Hillary said. "It just t-turned on and then th-they left."

Sam shook his head. "I hope you aren't going to blame this on those fairies," he exaggerated the word fairies as if it were a bad word.

Sam hadn't always disliked the mention of the little beasts. As a child, he grew up with fairies being talked about like they were your next-door neighbor. "How are the fairies today?" his mother would ask. "Did you leave the sugar water out for the fairies?"

He had always believed in them, up till the seventh grade. This, presumptively, had been the age when children stopped being children and also stopped believing in fantasy worlds. He realized that fairies were not to be discussed around other kids his age unless he wanted to be picked on and called ugly names like, 'Fairy'.

Sam opened the rear door, expecting George and Hillary to climb in. "I think this has been a rough day for all of us."

"But, dad," George whined.

"No buts," his dad said, pointing to the open door. "A light appearing in the middle of a swarm of bees cannot happen. It could have been the sun reflecting off one of the metal pieces on the casket."

George lowered his head in defeat. He knew his dad could have been right about a reflection. Why hadn't he thought of that conclusion? But the light had gone with the bees. If the light had been a reflection, then it would have stayed in one place.

"The light moved with the bees, dad," George said, trying to make his father understand. George doubted it would work.

"I'm sure you think you saw a light," Sam agreed, "but your mind can play strange tricks on you."

****

"C-could they be F-Fairies?" Hillary asked Mrs. Winstock. She leaned forward in her seat, attempting to pry an answer from her nanny. "You kn-know, v-visiting Na-Nana?"

Mrs. Winstock turned slightly and shook her head no. "Not now, Hillary," she said as Sam opened the driver's side door and got in.

Mrs. Winstock is the know-it-all of the fairy world; at least she seemed to be. Their Nana and she would talk to the little creatures every day when they worked in the yard. The two of them would give the fairies warnings when they were going to water the hedges surrounding the house. "Be careful, little ones," Nana would say, "a rainstorm is coming your way."

George stared out of the window the entire ride, playing with his tie. He rolled it up to his neck, and then let go, allowing it to unroll.

Hillary sat in her seat quietly, thinking about the swarm of bees. Could they be fairies? If they were fairies, then why visit her Nana's casket? And what had been shining in the center of the swarm?

The light within the bees bothered her for some reason. Her dad said it had to be a reflection and she knew there had to be things in the world that she had not witnessed. Could it have just been a reflection? Could a reflection move and she not understand how?

From the corner of her eye, she spied Mrs. Winstock's reflection on the passenger side window. She stared out into the nothingness as Hillary had done before. But could she be smiling? Hillary looked harder, trying to focus on the reflection, trying to ignore the background images flying past. Yes, Mrs. Winstock smiled larger than she had ever seen her smile making her face seem to light up. Why? Mrs. Winstock smiled the whole drive home as Hillary stared at her.

The truck pulled into their driveway. The white caliche driveway pathed its way to an old white farmhouse to the right, their house. Vines climbed up the side of the house as if trying to win a slow-paced race to the roof.

The shaggy grass looked as if it had not seen a lawnmower in about a month. A shed sat offset from the house, which held all of their dad's work tools and the riding lawnmower. Shingles were missing from the roof due to high winds over the years.

A lone, tall, leafless tree could be seen in the distance behind the shed, in the middle of the woods. Hillary and George watered the tree many times over the past year attempting to bring life back to it. Their Nana had told them the tree could not be cured with water because of some type of disease.

Sam parked the truck between the shed to the left and the house to the right. Hillary waited patiently in the back seat for her father to open her door. George opened his door and jumped carefully onto the ground. Hillary sat back, waiting patiently to tell George what she had seen.

George loosened his red tie and gulped fresh air as if he had not been able to breathe all day. Hillary impatiently scooted across the seat to exit on George's side, carefully stepping down from the truck.

Sam met Mrs. Winstock in front of the truck, helping her up the porch stairs leading to the white paint-flecked door.

"Thank you," she said as they walked up the stairs.

"Come on, children," Mrs. Winstock said from the top of the stairs. "You need to change out of your nice clothes."

"Coming," George said, walking toward the house. Hillary grabbed his hand and pulled on him. "What?"

"She sm-smiled the whole r-ride home," Hillary said softly.

"Okay?" George said. "People can smile."

"George, I haven't e-ever seen her sm-smile li-like that," she argued.

"Are you trying to say she is happy that Nana is gone?" George asked.

"I do-don't know," she said, looking up to the house. She didn't want to believe Mrs. Winstock would be happy that their Nana had died. She hadn't smiled the whole time until the ride home.

"What if she smiled about the bees?" George asked. They both looked in the direction of their father and Mrs. Winstock, entering the house.

"Are you coming inside?" their father asked, now leaning out of the door.

Hillary and George both walked hurriedly to the house. They had so many questions for Mrs. Winstock, but they had to be asked at the right time, without their father around.

****

The kids entered the house and George shut the door behind them. A stairway to the left of the front door led to their father's room. The room once belonged to their grandparents. Nana moved out of the room when his dad, his mother, Hillary, and he moved in.

Their Papa had died, sparking the move. They had been told that they needed to move because their Nana required help with the business. At the time, they didn't want to move, but their dad said Mrs. Winstock and Nana couldn't handle everything by themselves. They needed family close to them.

Moving from the big city of Austin, Texas, where tens of thousands of cars packed the roads, to the small city of Beeville, Texas, where only hundreds drove at one time, seemed strange. No sprawling buildings were glistening in the sunlight. The school turned out to be much smaller, with fewer kids.

The children passed through the tiny hallway into the kitchen where Mrs. Winstock had already filled a large pot with water and had it on the stove to boil for supper. They turned left in the kitchen and entered another hallway leading to the living room. Along this hallway were Nana's room to the left, Mrs. Winstock's room straight ahead, the bathroom, and then the children's room further down to the left. A few more feet and the hallway opened up to the large living room.

Their father had already gone upstairs to his room to change. Mrs. Winstock had gone to her room. "Is this the t-time, George?"

"We can ask her before dad comes down," George said, walking up to Mrs. Winstock's door. Hillary knocked on the old heavy wooden door and stood there with George hoping to get some information.

Mrs. Winstock opened the door. The hinges creaked. She still wore her funeral clothes. She hadn't had a chance to change yet, or she had been standing in her room waiting for the kids to question her. "Yes?" she asked.

"Why w-were you s-smiling in the t-truck, Mrs. Winstock?" Hillary stuttered through the tough question, scared to hear the answer.

"Smiling?" Mrs. Winstock asked, almost embarrassed.

"Yes," George said sternly. "Hillary told me you were staring out the window and smiling. I told her you were smiling because of the bees."

"Come in here," the old woman said, waving them in.

They did as she asked and walked in, shutting the door behind them. A bronze, antique lamp sitting on a table next to her pristine bed lit the room. The shades were drawn for privacy. Normally they were wide open, allowing the sunlight to brighten the room.

"I smiled because I am happy," she said. "Your grandmother was a dear friend, and I am sad for her passing, but today something happened, which you witnessed."

"The bees were f-fairies," Hillary said excitedly.

Mrs. Winstock smiled brightly. "No. They weren't fairies. They were normal bees, I am sure of it."

"The li-light," Hillary guessed again, hoping she had been right this time.

"The light," she said, giddily pointing at Hillary. "You telling me about the light made me happy. I don't know what it could have been, but I can tell you, the light had to be a sign. They are still watching, and they are still here."

"Come on, Mrs. Winstock," George said, rubbing the back of his neck. "Dad says they don't exist, and I believe him. I haven't seen one. He hasn't seen one."

"Oh," their nanny said, chuckling. "They exist. I have something for you two. Your grandmother has been working on something for years and I will show you tonight."

"Tonight?" George asked. "Why not now?"

"Because I have supper to cook, and your father will be down from his room shortly," she said, ushering them out of her room. "You need to get dressed in something more comfortable."

George opened the door and walked down the hallway. Hillary stopped as she walked out of the room and turned around. "The li-light is a g-good thing?"

"I think it is," Mrs. Winstock said, smiling.

With this answer, she turned to the left and ran down the hallway, to her room. She heard the creaking door shut as she entered the room with George.

"You get dressed in the bathroom this time," he said. "I got here first."

Hillary went to her dresser and pulled out some pajamas. "Fine."

****

22

They could smell the lovely aroma of pasta through the house. Excited, they quickly made their way to the table and sat down, waiting to pig out. They both looked toward Mrs. Winstock putting the last touches on her food. She had dressed in her normal clothes, a light-blue dress with white ruffles on the hem with a cooking apron with two big pockets. These pockets were known to hold some candy and other things.

She reminded the kids of a magician they had seen at school. If they asked for something Mrs. Winstock would reach in those big pockets and produce it. Tada. It seemed as if she knew what the children would ask for at any given moment in the day.

Sam walked down the stairs from his bedroom and made his way to the table. He wore a pair of blue jeans and a wrinkled white undershirt. By the look of his ruffled hair, they could tell he had not been feeling very well. "Are you ready to eat?" he asked.

"Dad?" Hillary asked. "Are y-you okay?"

Sam ran his fingers through his hair in frustration, placing a fake smile on his face. "Shouldn't I be asking if you two are okay?"

"Yeah," George said quietly, "but we see how you look."

Sam closed his eyes and sighed. "I'm sorry. You two are the greatest."

His words put a big smile on both Hillary and George's faces.

"Dinner time," Mrs. Winstock said, placing a big bowl of pasta in front of them. The red sauce smothered the white wormy noodles. She produced a bottle of ranch dressing out of a big pocket on her apron. "And here is the ranch dressing, George."

George filled his plate with pasta and then drizzled the white liquid over it, something his mom would do. "Not too much and not too little," she would say.

"Really?" Hillary asked George. She had tried ranch dressing once and couldn't understand why her mom and George liked it so much.

"What?" he asked, putting the lid back on. "It's good like this."

The four sat at the table in silence as they ate their food. George and Hillary ate their combination of noodles and sauce hurriedly because they couldn't wait to see the surprise Mrs. Winstock would show them. Sam ate slowly, as did Mrs. Winstock.

After dinner, they all helped clean up the mess. Sam and George started washing the dishes as Hillary and Mrs. Winstock put all the leftovers away in the fridge. The family loved eating leftover spaghetti.

"I'm going to retrieve something from my room," Mrs. Winstock said to Sam. "I think the kids will enjoy this."

Sam and George finished drying and putting the clean dishes away. Hillary sat at the table, waiting eagerly for whatever Mrs. Winstock had planned on showing them. Sam and George both sat at the table as the elderly woman exited her room.

She held a brown leather purse from the strap. George recognized this brown purse and knew it had belonged to his grandmother.

He vaguely remembered his Nana sitting outside with it once, when they were down visiting from Austin. His Papa had been alive at the time, Hillary had just started talking, and his mother was still very much a part of their family. She held Hillary while they all sat outside of this very house on the front porch.

His Nana pulled a book from it. He couldn't remember exactly what it looked like. Had the book been brown and tattered? He remembered asking her about the book, and she said she had been writing a book. He had asked her to read it to him, but she told him the book could not be read like a story, that it was a book about life in the woods; more of a field guide for people who can't see what's right in front of their faces.

George remembered accepting this as an answer and just left. Where did he go next? He couldn't remember. He probably played in the yard.

Sam pushed himself away from the table and stood up. "I am very sorry guys, but I have to go to the Johnson's house tonight for a little while."

"This late, Sam?" Mrs. Winstock asked, scrunching her eyebrows.

"Why do you have to go tonight, dad?" George asked, already knowing he would not be able to convince his father to stay. His father had been very distant for a long time, busying himself with work. Their fun time had been spent with their Nana and Mrs. Winstock. Now, it seemed their time would be spent with Mrs. Winstock, alone.

"I need to get things set up for the job tomorrow," Sam said, rustling George's hair. "I would like to show up tomorrow afternoon and start working on their yard instead of spending an hour in the heat, setting everything up. Nana wouldn't like a job to be on hold. You knew how she could be. Customer's first. I will be home in time to tuck you in bed."

Hillary jumped from her chair, ran to her dad, and gave him a big hug. George followed slowly, holding his head down sadly. He had hoped that his dad would have at least stayed a while longer.

They watched as Sam walked out of the door, shutting it behind him.

"Okay, kids," Mrs. Winstock said enthusiastically. "Time to find out what's in this bag."

Hillary and George both turned around and saw Mrs. Winstock sitting at the table with the leather purse sitting on top of the table. "Your grandmother asked me to show you something which she held dear to her heart."

"I remember that bag," George said, taking his seat back at the table. "There is a book in there, but I can't remember what it looks like."

She removed a large book bound in leather. A thin, gold trim surrounded the dirty brown hardcover. The pages within looked weathered and brittle. "This is a book your grandmother worked on for many years. She drew the pictures and described the fairies she always talked about."

It's about the things in the woods, George thought, as he remembered the conversation with his Nana. *It's about fairies, the things she never talked about with them.*

Mrs. Winstock opened the book to what seemed like a random page. "Ah, this is a mushroom fairy." She held up the book so they could see a rough drawing of a mushroom with small black, beady eyes and a wide smile. The mushroom fairy's stem separated into two legs so it could walk. Its cap reminded Hillary of a large, puffy hat. Its long, bony fingers seemed to be reaching out to them. This picture didn't resemble any fairy they had heard of in books or seen in the movies.

They weren't used to talking about fairies. Normally, their Nana and Mrs. Winstock would talk about the little creatures quietly, as if they didn't want the children to be a part of their conversation. They had never been shown a drawing of one.

"Is that w-what they really look like?" Hillary asked.

Mrs. Winstock placed the book down on the tabletop. "Not all of them. They aren't all nice either. Some can be very tricky and bad." She thumbed through the book until she came across a page that satisfied her. Hand scribed words covered the thick page without a picture. A name, Jenny Greenteeth had been written in beautifully scrawled letters. "For example, this little bugger called Jenny Greenteeth."

27

"J-Jenny Greent-teeth," Hillary said, leaning over the table. Her neck stretched like a turtle. "Her name is w-weird."

"According to your Nana," Mrs. Winstock continued, "she is a water fairy, a nymph, who preys on children who go near her waters. Children become trapped in her weeds and she pulls them under to drown them."

"Does she eat them?" George asked. He could imagine a pretty, blue fairy calling over some helpless child and then showing its green sharp teeth when the child least suspected it.

"No," Mrs. Winstock answered. "She just wants to play with them. She doesn't understand life the way we understand it. There is only one nymph per body of water, so this equals loneliness. No other being will go near her because she is so playful and curious. She doesn't ask permission to play; she just grabs."

This sent chills down Hillary's back. "I thought all fairies were nice."

"No," Mrs. Winstock said bluntly. "Unfortunately, they can be tricky. According to this book, your Nana has drawn out some pretty bad ones, but I won't get into that with you tonight."

"How did she know?" George asked, coming to a realization. "How did she know all of this? She could have been making this up as she went. There is no way for her to know what they looked like. She hadn't ever seen one."

"Are you sure?" Mrs. Winstock asked, raising an eyebrow.

"If she did, then she would have trapped them," George said. "to show dad, you know, to make him believe."

"It's funny that you said she would have to trap them. Your grandmother wrote about capturing fairies."

Mrs. Winstock flipped through the book again allowing the brown pages to fall upon one another. Blurred images flew quickly through their vision until she came toward a section at the end of the book.

"I think she wanted to enter the world of fairies," Mrs. Winstock smiled.

"You can g-go to the fairy w-world?" Hillary asked, surprised by this statement.

"Not only can you go to their world, but they can come into the human world as well." She reached in her pocket and pulled out a square cube of gum. She removed the paper and threw the gum in her mouth. She then rolled the paper into a ball, placing it in one of the big pockets on the apron.

"Wait a minute," George said, waving his hands in front of him. "If the fairies came into our world, wouldn't you be able to see their wings?" George asked.

"No," Mrs. Winstock answered, smacking her gum. "Legend says fairies that enter the realm of humans lose their wings and can only cross back to their realm if they are allowed entrance by a being of their world. That is the reason for the traps."

"So you catch a fairy and it takes you to their world?" George asked. "I don't believe that, Mrs. Winstock."

"Why is that, George?" she asked, knowing he could be skeptical regarding this topic. He had acquired a lot of his dad's

"How would you get there?" he asked, with his arms crossing his chest. "If everything is true that you are saying, then you would have to be shrunk down to the size of a bug."

"Exactly," Mrs. Winstock said, turning the book around to the children and pointed at a picture of mushrooms in a circle. "This is a fairy ring. You have to catch one, and then find the fairy ring. This ring is the portal from our world to theirs."

Hillary and George leaned forward to examine the finally detailed artwork of the mushrooms. Much time had gone into drawing each mushroom because each was different. Some had tall, pointy caps and others were flat.

After they both stared at the picture for some time, Mrs. Winstock thumbed through the book, turning the pages as if she were reading the book in reverse order. She came to a page and made an 'ah' sound. She pointed at the page she had come to, showing many pictures of elaborate traps. "She has many notes in this book about how to catch one of them. Each one has flaws, and none of them caught anything."

Some sketches had been drawn with a shaky hand on two pages. A tiny spool of thread holding a tiny door open on a soda can seem to be one of the traps Mrs. Winstock had referred to. Another picture depicted an open box of toothpicks. A net had been drawn under a table with a peppermint candy as the bait. An open Hershey candy bar had been drawn, but not finished because no discernible trap could be seen.

"What did she use for bait?" George asked. "I see a peppermint candy and a Hershey bar, but I don't see how the fairies could be caught by those."

Mrs. Winstock nodded her head and said, "She tried cotton candy, flowers, syrup, and many other things. There seemed to always be a problem." A small pink bubble slowly protruded from her mouth. The bubble stretched and then popped. Mrs. Winstock pulled the gum back into her mouth and continued to chew.

Hillary sat straight in her chair, wanting to hear why her Nana's traps didn't work. "W-What?"

"How could you grab a little fairy while they ate?" she asked them. She blew another small bubble. "Nothing would hold them there long enough for you to snatch it up. They would simply fly away and never be seen again."

"What about gum?" George asked nonchalantly. "Not the dry kind, but the wet kind, after you have chewed it up?"

In the middle of blowing a bubble, Mrs. Winstock spat it out of her mouth, surprised by what George said. Mrs. Winstock grabbed into the air, attempting to catch it, but failed.

Hillary thought it looked like a jellyfish flying across the room. It landed on the floor and deflated as a small hole ripped in the side.

"Now that's a good idea," she said, pushing off the chair, a little embarrassed that she spat her gum halfway across the room. Mrs. Winstock bent over, holding her back, as she plucked the gum from the ground. "You have to excuse me for doing that. Your idea surprised me."

Mrs. Winstock sat back down and they talked for another hour about the fairies. How they lived in trees, flowers, rocks, and water. She explained that fairies could look like any bug. George realized that he would not be stepping on bugs again.

After the discussion, Mrs. Winstock guided the children off to bed, knowing they would have great dreams tonight. After getting dressed into their pajamas, Hillary laid in her bed while George laid in his. As soon as Hillary pulled the covers over her body the front door shut, echoing to their room.

"D-dad's home," Hillary said excitedly.

George rolled his eyes at her stout observation.

"Hello, Mrs. Winstock," they heard Sam say in a tired voice. "Are the kids asleep?"

"Think he'll tuck us in?" George asked.

"Shhh," Hillary hushed him. "I want to hear them."

"Why?" George asked rudely. "Why do you want to snoop?"

"I see you have mom's book out," they heard Sam say.

"Oh no," Hillary said while covering her mouth. "She left the book out."

"Yes, I did," Mrs. Winstock responded. "And they need that right now."

"You know how I feel about the fairy stories," he said in an exasperated voice.

"And you weren't here to listen to it," Mrs. Winstock said. Hillary and George heard Mrs. Winstock shut her bedroom door.

"Hey, kids," Sam said in an almost upbeat voice while walking into their room. "Are you ready to be tucked in?"

They nodded their heads enthusiastically. Ever since their mother had disappeared from her car, their father seemed to have gone with her. Quality time with their father became rare. He spent most of his days tending to clients' yards and avoiding his children.

Sam reached down, kissed George on the forehead, and told him goodnight. He then walked over to his daughter.

"D-Dad?" Hillary asked, wanting to get her father's attention.

"Yes?" he asked.

"George had a gr-great idea," she said excitedly.

George immediately sat up in his bed, glaring at her. He shook his head behind his father's back. He feared what his dad would say to him if he found out about the fairies. He mouthed the word 'No'. She didn't pay any attention to him and completely ignored that he had said anything.

"What is it, Hillary?" Sam asked her, turning around to see George sitting up in bed. Sam smiled at him tiredly.

"Use g-gum to c-catch fairies," she said proudly.

Those words caused George to squint his eyes together, waiting for his father to scold him. He knew his father didn't believe in fairies and could easily get a little aggravated about the subject. They had been told over and over 'hunting fairies

33

is ridiculous'. They did not exist. They had been told of his nightly excursions in the woods trying to find one.

"Gum? Fairies?" is all Sam said. He let out a small snicker. "Really?"

"Yeah," George said quickly. He needed a quick answer before he went on about how the fairies never existed and how it is a waste of their time. "I only wanted to finally prove to Hillary that fairies are only in your imagination. If a fairy won't get stuck in gum then how else can you prove it?"

Sam smiled. "George. I tried catching those little, invisible beings at Hillary's age. I tried everything and it didn't work. The book about fairies had been your Nana's life work. Unfortunately, they don't exist. It would be impossible for those little beings to exist in our woods without being seen?"

"W-Why don't you b-believe in them?" Hillary asked.

"That is a story for another time," their father said, uncomfortably. "I wish they existed, I really do, but they don't."

Hillary glared at her brother as their father tucked them into bed. She didn't understand why George would say that he would try to prove they didn't exist. She became angry.

Sam walked from the room pulling the door closed behind him.

George lay back down in his bed and stared at the ceiling. He didn't know what to say. "Why did you tell dad about my idea?" Hillary didn't answer him. She gave him the silent treatment because he had betrayed her. "I'm sorry for saying fairies don't exist, but you know how dad is with this whole fairy thing, and I don't know if I believe in them." Still, no answer came. He soon closed his eyes and nodded off to sleep.

****

Sam shut their bedroom door and walked into the living room to stand in front of the unlit fireplace. He stared lovingly at a picture of his vanished wife. A picture of his mother stood beside his wife's.

"They're both very beautiful," Mrs. Winstock said from behind him, sneaking quietly out of her room.

"Yes, they were," Sam said, lowering his head.

Mrs. Winstock walked quietly into the living room adorned with paintings of landscapes from abroad. "Sam, you need to stop living in the past. It's been nearly a year and now your mother has passed on as well. Your children need you."

"I'm here for them," he said, denying the fact he hardly spent any time with them in the last year. He became wrapped up in his work and the thought of his wife.

"Sam, I'm leaving," she said, sitting down in her favorite chair in the corner, beneath the painting of the woods behind the house.

"Leaving?" Sam asked as if surprised. "My mother, your friend, just passed away and now you want to leave. How do you think that will make the children feel?"

"It's time for me to go, Sam," she said. "I am more of a hindrance to the relationship you should have with Hillary and George. The longer I'm here, the more you will pull away

35

from them. You spend so much time on the job as it is. You need to be with them and allow them to be themselves. Time is an important thing for their ever-growing mind. They need a father, not some old withered-up woman."

"I know," Sam said sadly. "I just see their mother in them every day. It's very hard sometimes. She means so much to me."

"If you are going through this much pain, just imagine how much pain they're going through."

Sam lowered his head and sighed deeply. He reluctantly asked, "When are you planning on leaving?"

"I might be leaving tomorrow," Mrs. Winstock said.

"Tomorrow?" Sam questioned in a higher-pitched voice.

"I have written a letter which explains my circumstances. I will place it on the mantel above the fireplace. I will talk to the children tomorrow afternoon and let them know why I am leaving. "

"The kids get told in person and I get a letter?" Sam asked. "Great."

"You won't understand if I tell you," Mrs. Winstock said.

"Try me," Sam said.

Mrs. Winstock stood and walked to the mantel with Sam. She stood by his side and placed a small hand on his shoulder. "Do you know what the kids are doing tomorrow?"

"No," Sam said.

"They are going to go hunt for fairies," she said.

"I take it they will be trying the gum?" he asked.

"It's a very good idea," she said. "I don't know why your mom or I didn't think of that. Or you."

"My mother had me hunting fairies at their age. I spent all that time in the woods looking for things that do not exist."

"How do you know they don't exist?" Mrs. Winstock asked, forcing her voice to stay calm.

"I have never seen them."

"Your mother built that wall surrounding the woods with your father because she believed in them. Shouldn't that be enough?"

The brick wall that surrounded two acres of land, designated Fairydom, by his mother had been built by his father. A gate guarding the entrance into Fairydom stood at the end of a pebbled walkway leading inside. Sam had never understood why his father or mother would do such a thing for creatures they had never seen. "I guess you have to have faith," his father had said to him long ago when asked about the fairies.

"There are things out there you cannot see or explain, Sam. There are also things right in front of your face which you refuse to see," she said, raising her eyebrows. "The once beautiful yard has become neglected. The weeds are overrunning it. The hedges are bushy and the trees are growing out of control. Take some time and help the children find their father again, Sam. Let them help you work in the yard. Your children need you."

Sam gazed at his wife in the sketch. "It seems I have forgotten to be a father since she vanished," Sam said as tears welled in his eyes.

"Go with them tomorrow and help them find the fairies within the enclosed sanctuary," Mrs. Winstock said, almost whispering it to him. "Maybe you will find yourself."

Sam continued to stand there, hearing her words of wisdom.

"It's time for me to retire. Goodnight." She placed the letter on the mantle between the pictures. She then walked into the hallway, leading to her bedroom.

Sam shook his head while gawking at the letter. He held back the desire to tear it open and read the contents. Instead, he threw his last words into the emptiness of the room. "But they don't exist."

Chapter Three
The Secret

The front door slammed, jostling Sam awake from a restless sleep. He had once again dreamed about his wife in a deep dark cave reaching out to him. This dream had come to be his normal sleeping prison he found himself in every night since his wife went missing.

At night, as he closed his eyes, she began calling to him, screaming in the distance. The darkness engulfed the scene around him. He could see himself standing in blackness while his wife's voice echoed all around him. He tries to talk, but something in his throat does not allow sound out. A sound of laughter, from some unknown voice, would echo as well. A woman would start laughing, but not his wife's laugh. This laugh struck him as being sinister. Terror. Fear. He would run into the blackness but never get anywhere. She would then appear, with her back to him. The long, flowing cloth surrounding her moved in the windless darkness. She then turned to him, revealing his wife, laughing that malevolent cackle.

Her normal deep emerald eyes would change to a milky-yellow color. Her pupils would narrow, resembling cat eyes. Her long hair would fall out, and her beautiful face would grow gold scales as her head narrowed, turning into what seemed like a dragon's head right out of a medieval drawing.

She snapped her powerful jaws, now filled with large serrated teeth. Her tongue would lash out. He tried to scream as always and nothing would ever come out.

He tried reaching for her, not fearing the dragon's head atop her body. She would always fall as if the black space gave way beneath her. Her arms reached out to him as he saw her body shrink in size as if falling but shrinking at the same time. He could never make out what exactly happens to her. He would reach to her and wake up.

He would never follow her. He could never reach her. Only blinding light would enter his eyes as he woke in the morning. The dream always seemed to last from the time he fell asleep to the time he woke up.

He found himself under a blanket his mother made long ago. Small diamond shape patterns of multiple colors had been sewn together to create the large blanket. He had fallen asleep again, fully clothed, in the old brown recliner in front of his wrinkleless bed.

Every night, since his wife's disappearance, he slept there, looking fixedly at the bed they had once shared. Each night, he grabbed the blanket and sat on the old recliner thinking if tonight would be the night he would be able to hold his wife in his dreams. If only he could tame the dragon she had become. He knew that scenario would never happen, but he always hoped.

"Thanks, guys," he said sarcastically. He pushed the blanket off, knowing that his children had slammed the door.

He could hear their laughter growing fainter as they ran to the woods.

He stood from the recliner and folded the blanket, placing it over the back of his makeshift bed. He walked by his bed and placed a hand on it. How he wished he could sleep in it. He knew he would sleep better, but could not bring himself to lie there comfortably, knowing that his wife could be out there somewhere.

He walked to the one window in the room and moved the blackout curtains aside. Sam squinted his eyes from the blinding morning sunlight cascading into the room. From this window, he could see the entire backyard. His parked truck sat to the left, the shed to the left of that. The neglected yard peered back at him with disdain. Tall, un-mowed grass danced in the slight wind as if dancing to soundless music. The once white rock wall his parents built for the fairies stood as a reminder of every failure he had as a child.

Behind the wall stood the brown, dying trees that had once been so majestic. His mother called it the land of fairies, Fairydom. Sam couldn't remember a time when the woods were as majestic as his mother made them out to be.

The woods had only grown darker over time. No matter how much it rained, no matter how much he attempted to bring life back to the woods, they were a waste of land. The only hope he ever had for the woods had been the sparse green areas that were not affected by whatever disease plagued it. One tree stood tall amongst all the other ones in the woods. His father called it the "Moving Tree".

His grandparents uprooted the tree around sixty years ago when they were building the house they live in now. His grandmother would tell the story of how she saved the tree from being killed. She asked her father to uproot it and move it into the woods and that is exactly what he had done.

To Sam, this feat seemed unimaginable. The tree had to be at least fifty feet tall and just as wide near the bottom of the crown. The sparse foliage on the tree mimicked the surrounding woods. The disease seemed to have infected the tree many years ago but had not fully engulfed it. His mother cared deeply for this old tree, probably due to its history with the family. This had been the only tree she cared for in the woods and the only plant he knew she could not save.

Vines grew around a birdbath in the middle of the yard. They were like snakes, trying to choke the life out of a helpless stone bird sitting on top of the fountain. Water had once flowed from its beak, but the water pump had gone out.

A dead tree stump larger than the base of the birdbath had been left in the ground. His mother refused to remove the stump for some odd reason. Regardless of how dead it looked or how it took away the possible beauty of her perfectly groomed lawn, his mom revered it. He remembered seeing her pat it every once in a while with a loving hand as if she could persuade to come back to life.

His mother would never have allowed the yard to be kept in this manner if she hadn't been so sick. She would have been outside picking weeds from the flowerbeds, trimming the hedges, and preventing vines from growing on the side of the house. "We wouldn't want to upset the fairies now, would we?" he remembered his mother saying daily.

"Fairies," Sam whispered. "What a waste of my childhood." He thought back to all the chasing he did as a child. He would set traps, search spider webs, and hide behind trees for hours. Nothing ever worked. Nothing would work because fairies only existed in the minds of people who wanted to believe.

He watched his children ring a bell attached to an iron gate. The gate, the entrance to Fairydom, had been installed between two sections of the wall. According to his parents, whoever entered Fairydom must ring the bell. "It gives them notice," his mother had said. Hillary and George opened the gate and closed it behind them, disappearing into the woods.

Sam let the curtain go, darkening the room. It suited the mood he would be putting his family in later. A few days prior he had gone to Mr. Drake's place of business, Statuesque, an old shop downtown on Main Street. The name of the business plainly did not describe Mr. Drake. The short, chubby, balding man waddled out from behind the counter and greeted him.

This man had attempted to buy the land over the years and his mother would turn him down with a slammed door in his face. Sam understood why she didn't want to sell. Her fantasy of the fairies living in the woods had become an obsession for her. Even though she watched the woods slowly turn brown, she still felt an obligation to return the woods from the brink of death. She would have never given up on the woods, but Sam knew when to call it quits, and this had to be the time.

Mr. Drake sold lifelike representations of the fairies his mother had described. Had everyone around him been obsessed with these little beings? Is this why he wanted the lands behind the house? If so, would he go running around the woods and attempt to find a real fairy?

Sam could remember the grin Mr. Drake had on his face as Sam offered to sell the land to him. It reminded him of a victor in a long-fought battle of wills. This man had won. Sam had surrendered the spoils of the battle for a price.

The woods had been dying gradually over time. For this reason and this reason alone, or so Sam told himself, is the reason he had to sell the woods to Mr. Drake. He had not reached this decision without doubt, but he knew it had to be done. Mrs. Winstock, George, and Hillary would need to be told today, and he didn't feel ready to tell the people he loved. Could he be feeling guilty for doing this? Had he made a rash decision in the grief of losing his mom a year after he lost his wife?

Sam turned from the window as a whistle shouted from downstairs. Mrs. Winstock must have just finished brewing her strong sweet tea. Sam took a shower and then dressed, ready to face the dark day. He exited his room, walking down the narrow steps to the kitchen. He could hear Mrs. Winstock humming a tune in perfect pitch. How would he tell her what he has decided to do?

At the bottom of the stairs, he looked to his left to see Mrs. Winstock sitting at the round kitchen table as if waiting for him to arrive. "Tea is ready," she said, gesturing to a teacup placed on the table in front of his chair. Light steam wisped from the cup.

"Good morning," Sam said, walking toward Mrs. Winstock. A jar of Peter Pan peanut butter grabbed his attention. It sat on the counter with the lid off. Ziploc bags were next to the jar along with the bread, fully open. He shook his head and sighed. This irritated him. The kids should know better than to leave out a mess like this before running into the woods to play.

"Good morning, Sam," Mrs. Winstock said, cheerfully. "I wouldn't worry about cleaning that up. I am going to make a peanut butter sandwich in a bit." She gestured to the chair which had been pushed out from the table. "Please have a seat. I would like to discuss a few things if you don't mind."

"When are they going to learn?" he asked, screwing the lid back on the jar, not wanting bugs to find their way into it.

"They didn't do that," Mrs. Winstock said with her back to him. She lifted the teacup to her lips. "I made those sandwiches before they went into the woods."

Sam sighed. He tilted the jar to see the green pixie on the jar flying with his arms open. Hillary had once told him that this picture depicted the king of the peanut butter fairies. This made him laugh. Even now, he smiled at the memory.

He placed the jar back on the counter and closed the bread with a quick twist. He turned to the table as Mrs.

Winstock slurped loudly on her tea. *Could she be trying to agitate me first thing in the morning?* he thought

He sat at the table, slowly raising the cup of tea to his mouth. This had to be the darkest tea she had ever made. It almost looked like freshly brewed coffee. Smells from the liquid caused his nostrils to open wide, taking every bit of the relaxing aroma.

There seemed to be so many smells to take in; mint, honey, and some other smells he could not identify. Sam happily sipped it slowly as Mrs. Winstock watched, waiting for his approval. "The best tea you ever made," Sam said, enjoying the aftertaste. "Mint and honey don't seem like they go together, but you made the perfect combination."

"Of course," she replied, sipping at her cup again.

He placed his teacup on the small plate, opened his mouth to tell her about the land. He reluctantly closed it and then opened it again; and with hesitation, closed it. How would he be able to tell her about the woods? She would be leaving, so it might not affect her too badly. Maybe she had changed her mind about leaving.

Over the last year, she had left the letter five times, telling Sam that she needed to leave. The next day after being gone for a while, she would show back up and explain things weren't working out as she had planned. She apologized for inconveniencing them; they would laugh about it, and go on with their day. Something about this time seemed as if she would leave. She seemed different with a type of finality to the way she spoke to him.

Sam sipped his tasty tea and finally decided to start the conversation. "Mrs. Winstock, you don't have to say anything. I know you want to stay. And we would love for you to stay. This is what, the sixth time you have tried leaving us?"

Mrs. Winstock smiled and bowed her head, almost embarrassed. "Yes, Sam, I would love to stay here with you and the children."

"Then it's settled," Sam said. "You don't have to go on with any further discussion."

"It seems you have become accustomed to my departures," Mrs. Winstock said, frowning. "I'm sorry, but this time I am going. Last night had been a bit of an eye-opener for me."

"What?" Sam asked, almost harshly. "You're actually leaving?"

"It's the children, Sam," she said.

"What did they do?" Sam asked, surprised by her statement.

"They did nothing," she said, giggling. She took another sip, letting these words seep in. "It's time for me to go. These children need you now more than they ever did. They lost their mother, a very important person in their little lives. In a way, you also let them lose their father. Now their grandmother has passed. Come back to them, Sam, they need you."

"So we're going to continue the conversation from last night?" he asked.

"No," Mrs. Winstock said, taking a sip. "I just want to ensure you understand me and hear me."

"Where will you go?" Sam asked, realizing that she had been serious. This woman, who had been in his life longer than anyone alive, is leaving him. He had started to feel every bit of his emotion rise up in him. His wife had left him, his mother had passed away, and now Mrs. Winstock dropped this bombshell on him.

****

Mrs. Winstock arrived on a sweltering July night after his twelfth birthday. The month had set record highs with a drought that had been ongoing for months. The woods were mostly green, but not to the majestic beauty his mom talked about. The creek that ran through the woods had mostly dried up, only leaving small puddles.

His dad had poked his head in the front door and said, "I think I smell rain."

Both his mom and he ran to the door and sniffed the night air. To this day, the smell of rain remained his favorite smell, a musky earth scent.

His father had stood in the middle of the yard looking up to the heavens. His mom had walked into the yard to stand next to her husband. Sam watched them with admiration, as his dad waved him over to join them. Sam ran to them as the sky released the much-needed rain upon the land.

All three of them had danced in the rain, stomping in the forming mud puddles. Sam had fallen to the ground and rolled in the cool water. They continued to dance for what seemed like hours. He laughed at his parents as they ran down the old dirt road in front of their house.

Lightning flashed across the sky, illuminating their surroundings. As he ran to his parents, he noticed that they were standing in the middle of the dirt road, not celebrating anymore. The lightning flashed again, revealing a figure walking toward them. The figure walked casually as if the rain did not affect her.

"Can we help you?" his father had asked, wiping the rain from his face.

"I am Mrs. Winstock," the figure said. She wore the same large eyeglasses she wears to this day. Her large straw hat, with soaking wet flowers sewn to a blue ribbon, had blocked the rain from hitting her face. She held a single leather bag to her chest. "I am here regarding the ring."

Sam's mother had looked at her husband and nodded her head. Sam had been ushered in the house by his father. They both dried off and got dressed. As they came out of their rooms, Mrs. Winstock sat at the kitchen table, drenched in rainwater. His mother stood over the stove brewing tea.

"I have been walking all night," Mrs. Winstock had said. "I do hope I have the right house. I am sure I do, but something seems...off."

"I assure you," his mother had said placing her hand on top of Mrs. Winstock's, "You are in the right place."

Sam had wondered and still wondered to this day if his parents knew this strange woman who had just appeared. Had his mother been expecting her? Why did his mom act as if she owed something to Mrs. Winstock?

"Oh good," Mrs. Winstock had said. "When do I get to-?"

"Not here," his mom had said, looking at Sam.

His mother had waved him over and introduced Mrs. Winstock as the new nanny. She had been offered a room in the house which she gladly took. She had remained with the family for twenty-five years, outlasting his father and mother.

****

"I have a place to go," Mrs. Winstock said, snapping Sam out of his memories. She took another sip of her warm, mint-honey sweet tea. "Drink up, Sam, before it gets cold. It tastes odd when the warmth goes away."

Sam looked at the cup of tea he held in his trembling hand. "The children will miss you."

She smiled brightly. "I will miss them. Your children sparked a life inside of me I thought died long ago. Hillary will get over her stuttering. It's just going to take time to get over her traumatic loss. George needs you. He is so creative. At one time you had the same creativeness and imagination. Your mother told me that long ago."

Sam sat back in his chair. "My mother wanted me to hunt for fairies in the yard. She wanted me to chase things that never existed."

"That is your belief, Sam," Mrs. Winstock said, taking the last sip from her teacup. "Let your children believe, Sam.

Right now, George is out there setting a trap he came up with all on his own."

"The gum," Sam sighed, taking his last sip.

"Yes," Mrs. Winstock said, picking up the teapot. She asked, "Another cup of tea?"

Sam pushed his cup forward, watching the steam rise and fade away into the air as she filled his cup. "George told me he didn't believe in fairies."

"He doesn't want you mad at him," Mrs. Winstock said.

"Mad?" Sam asked curiously. "I wouldn't be mad. I just don't want him to go through what I went through. The bullying alone had been enough to not believe in them."

"I am sorry for what you went through," Mrs. Winstock said. "Let them believe while they're children. Time will come soon enough when they will not believe, and they will have a family of their own."

Sam sighed. He had been outwitted by Mrs. Winstock. He didn't have a rebuttal. He didn't see the point in arguing over these fairies. Why argue over something which doesn't exist. "So, the trap is gum?"

"He calls it sticky snare," Mrs. Winstock said, smiling brightly. "Clever little boy. Gum had never entered my mind. Why? Who knows? To simple if you ask me."

"Well," Sam said, taking a sip of his tea. "I would have to agree with you, but I have seen a lot of gum on the ground in my life and I have never seen a single insect in one. So maybe this will be the time they realize fairies don't exist."

Mrs. Winstock shook her head. She gave up long ago trying to argue the fact about fairies. "They would enjoy your company in the woods," Mrs. Winstock encouraged him while nodding her head in the direction of the woods. She sighed slightly and lowered her head. "I didn't want to say much about this subject, but I feel it must be brought up."

Sam eyed her with caution. "And what might that be?"

She took a large gulp of tea. "The woods."

"What about them?" he asked, stiffening his hand around the teacup. Could she know he would be selling them? Of course, she knew. She knew everything. He felt the need to reveal his dirty little secret. First, he had to sell the idea to the one person who could crush him with a simple look. "You already know they're dying. For some reason, they seem to be becoming darker over the last year."

"Selling the woods is a bad idea," she said with no qualm.

Sam felt as if he had been punched in the gut. How did she know about the woods being sold? This explained why the lid had been off of the peanut butter, the bread left open, and the loud obnoxious slurping. He placed the teacup on the small plate causing it to clank.

"Your mother would be very disappointed. Your wife would be horrified."

"Mrs. Winstock," Sam said, standing from the table. He needed to get his thoughts together after she had beaten him to the punch. "I don't know how you found out. But you must know how depressing it is to look out my window every morning and see the trees become more diseased. Before it gets too bad, I need to sell the land for a good price"

"Money. Bah," she said, eyeing him keenly. She asked, "I bet that old Mr. Drake finally talked you into it?"

"I went to him," Sam said crudely. He didn't like himself very much right now. "He offered me a very good price. He noticed the trees were dying too, and his offer seems to be a generous one."

"Do you know what that man is going to do to it?" Mrs. Winstock asked. "He is a bad man, Sam. You can't trust him."

"He has already told me the trees will stay because he needed them for something," Sam said, sitting up now.

"Then why are you selling the woods?" she challenged, raising an eyebrow. "If he isn't going to flatten them, then you will have to see the trees every day anyway."

Sam looked down. She had him backed into a corner. How would explain that he didn't want to deal with the woods any longer? How would he tell her that the woods didn't mean that much to him? He wanted to get rid of that memory from his childhood.

"You can't run away from your childhood," she said as if reading his mind. "You can't run away from your adulthood either."

"A part of me wants him to destroy the woods," Sam said angrily. "I can't do it, so I figured I would give it to the person who might do it for me."

"You'll get your wish," Mrs. Winstock said, grabbing his hand gently. "You don't know people like that. As soon as you sign the papers, he will have bulldozers ready to plow the land. Do you even know what's in those woods?"

"Fairies don't exist, Mrs. Winstock," Sam said, removing his hand from hers. He turned away from her, not wanting to see the hurt in her eyes. "I can't manage this house, a business, the children, and those woods. Now that you're leaving, I am glad I am selling the land. I really wouldn't be able to do it all."

Sam had twisted the knife, causing Mrs. Winstock to pause her needless attack on him. She didn't have the right to tell him what he could sell or couldn't sell. These woods didn't belong to her anyway.

"It's about the creek, about the memories, and yes about the fairies," she finally said. Sam could hear the sadness in her tone. "Think about what you are doing, Sam. Think about your children. Why would your mom build a wall if it wouldn't be to protect anything?"

"She had my father build that wall to protect what she believed to live in there," Sam said, turning back to Mrs. Winstock. He could feel his face flush. "Her delusion of little beings inhabiting the trees made her a crazy old woman."

"Bite your tongue, Sam," Mrs. Winstock chastised him. "Your mother knew more about those woods than you will ever know."

Sam, taken aback by her words, never heard her sound so angry. "She's not here now is she? She passed the land on to me, to manage how I see fit."

Mrs. Winstock lowered her head in surrender. "Sam, I just want you to think about the decision you have made.

Please don't sign those papers tomorrow." She stood from the chair and walked out of the room, leaving him standing alone to ponder over what she had said.

"So much for the secret," Sam said to himself. He gulped down the last of his tea. "I guess the children need to be told."

He walked across the kitchen to the backdoor. When he got outside, he looked around at the tall grass waving around in its silent dance to celebrate the new day. The morning felt crisp as if full of life. He walked down the creaking wooden steps, stepping onto the pebbled pathway, which had been covered by invasive weeds. The pebbles crunched under his feet as he stepped forward toward the iron gate.

He passed the shed and the water fountain. The feeling of dread came over him. He wanted to turn around and go back into the house, avoiding the conversation he needed to have with his children.

The woods before him looked darker than they did yesterday. Dried, brown leaves held onto the tree branches behind the wall. Inside the woods were his children who were going to be truly hurt by the news he brought them. They needed to know and now seemed to be a better time than never.

CHAPTER FOUR
STICKY SNARE

George closed the gate before they ventured down the narrow trail leading into the woods. His idea of sticky snare had to prove to Hillary fairies didn't exist or prove to his father that they did. He remained on the thin line of belief, needing to see them for himself.

"Did you b-bring the g-gum?" Hillary asked, walking slightly ahead of George. She wanted to see a fairy and her excitement had shown across her face.

"Yes," George said. "I have it right here." He pulled out a cubed piece of gum from his pocket with white paper folded around it. George had pulled this cube of gum from his dresser drawer, remnants from the previous Halloween tour around town.

George freed the gum from its paper prison and placed it in his mouth, starting to chew it. The watermelon flavor exploded in his mouth. If it weren't for the gummy texture, he would have sworn he ate an actual slice of watermelon.

They walked on the trail until it started to curve to the right. George stopped walking and pointed into the woods at the end of the trail. He said, "We are going through there."

"W-Why through here?" Hillary asked, looking in the dense trees. She could see thorns on some of the trees. Flat, green, oval-shaped cacti had grown in clumps a little further in.

She knew that each of the cactus pads had thorny spines sticking out of them which would hurt if she happened to accidentally brush up against one.

"There's a clearing on the other side of the cactus," George said. "It looks like it's going to block us, but it's two separate bunches. You can walk between them."

"How do you know about that?" Hillary asked, looking back at her big brother.

"I found it a few months ago when I came out here exploring."

George went first, pushing small limbs out of his way with Hillary following closely behind. The trees weren't twisted together as it had seemed. After a duck here and a dodge there, they were through to the cactus. The cactus stood in two separate bunches with a large enough space to go between them, just as George had said.

After the cactus, George pulled a limb back from its natural position and looked back to Hillary. "So what do you think?"

Hillary passed George and stopped abruptly as she entered the open area. Her mouth fell slack as her eyeballs rolled around in her head, taking in the beautiful sight before her. George hadn't described it to her and she couldn't be sure if he would have been able to. The beauty amazed her.

The open area had been covered by a canopy of tree limbs, hiding it from above. Beams of sunlight made their way through small openings in the canopy reaching the densely populated yellow flowers covering the ground. She noticed how quiet the clearing seemed as if the canopy of trees had created a field of silence.

"It's g-great," Hillary said, radiating with happiness.

"Now, do you think this would be a great place to catch a fairy?" George asked excitedly.

"Yeah," Hillary said, stepping forward. George placed an arm in front of Hillary, stopping her from going any further.

"You stay here," he said. "I don't want you stepping on the flowers."

Hillary pointed to the center of the flowers and pouted. "But I want to go over there,"

"I found this place," he said. "I don't want you stepping on them. Do you think the fairies would appreciate a human stomping on their flowers?"

"N-No," she said, crossing her arms and puffing out her lower lip.

"Wait here and don't touch anything," he said, taking his first step into the flowers. He pushed the flowers aside with the side of his foot, being careful to not step on a single one.

"What are you d-doing?" Hillary asked as George stopped after ten steps.

"I'm setting the trap," George said, putting his index finger to his lips. "Now, shhh."

After a few more chomps on the gum, he pulled it out of his mouth, squishing it in between his fingers. Satisfied with the disc shape, he pulled the gum apart until it tore to the center. He then placed it carefully around the base of one yellow flower. With the trap set, he smiled at the thought of a hapless fairy coming along and taking a bite of his sticky snare.

The sticky snare had been his idea and he felt that the gum would either prove or disprove the fantasy which had consumed his Nana. The Book of Fairies would either be shown to have been a real depiction of fairies or it could prove that his grandmother had a vast imagination. He hoped it to be true, but deep down he doubted they would catch anything.

How tall were the fairies? No mention of their size had been written in the book. He hadn't thought of that till right now. What if they can't be caught with gum? What if they were the size of a human and remained invisible until they wanted to be seen? Could that explain why no one could catch them?

"Hurry, G-George," Hillary whispered as if something could hear her. "They w-won't come if we're h-here."

"I'm on my way back," George said. He easily walked back to her along the same path he had made and then turned around to admire just how clever he was. A path easily led straight to the flower where his sticky snare had been set. "I guess we can find the gum when we come back to check on it. The path leads right to it."

"Can I p-pick a f-flower for dad?" Hillary asked.

"No," George answered abruptly. "I don't think that would be smart right now. We can pick one later when we come back to check the trap."

Hillary agreed and they navigated the woods back to the trail. "When do we come b-back to check on the t-trap?"

"We can go play at the creek," George said, exiting the dense woods onto the trail.

"I'm k-king of the hill," Hillary said, playfully pushing George. She ran left, down the trail leading to the creek.

"Hey," George said, running after her. He let her run ahead of him, deciding to allow her to be King or Queen of the hill, at least for a little while. They had played this game on a hill dubbed Fairy Mountain, across the creek.

Hillary immediately stopped when she arrived at the bank of the water. White rocks from the size of a balled-up fist to the size of peas were scattered around the creek's edge. She looked suspiciously into the water, watching the crystal clear stream flow gently by. Clumps of green grass at the bottom of the creek waved like flags in wind. The width of the creek reached only a few feet across and about knee-deep. Their dad had told them that the creek had stayed clear due to all of the rocks at the bottom, acting as a filtration system.

"Why did you stop?" asked George, stopping beside her.

"Jenny Greent-teeth," she responded.

"She's just a story," George said. "How many times have you been down here? How many times did you see a lonely fairy wanting to pull you into the water?"

"None," she answered timidly, not taking her eyes off the slow-moving water. Three stones crested the surface of the flowing water creating a pathway. These stones had been placed in the water at Mrs. Winstock's request years ago. She had convinced their dad it would make it easier for the children to cross so they wouldn't get wet.

"Exactly," he said, stepping on the first stone. "No Jenny Greenteeth. Come on."

Hillary watched George hop easily from the second and third stone to dry land on the other side. Why didn't he care about getting eaten by Jenny Greenteeth? She wished she could be brave like her brother. Could the water fairy just be a story? She stepped on the first stone and looked into the water again. Nothing moved in the water except for the grass and a lone leaf floating on top. The leaf twirled in the slow current, bouncing from the shore to the stepping stone, finally making its way to some unknown destination downstream.

Hillary gained courage and hopped onto the second and then the third stones, finally jumping safely to the other side. The vile fairy had not been there to grab her.

Fairy Mountain resembled a miniature hill, about six feet tall, made from rocks and dirt. According to their Nana, their Papa had created it with the dirt and rocks dug out of the creek. George always stood on top, proclaiming to the king.

"Come on, slowpoke," George taunted her as he started to climb the mountain.

Hillary proved to be faster. She ran at the mountain and leaped onto the side, crawling to the top. George smiled as she passed him, allowing his sister to be Queen of the Hill.

"I am K-King of the Hill," she yelled triumphantly, raising her arms in the air as her blonde hair moved slightly in the wind.

"*Queen* of the Hill," George corrected, looking up at her. "Only boys can be kings."

"W-Whatever," she said. "I am the w-winner."

"Okay," George agreed. "You got me."

Hillary lowered her arms and watched her brother monkey crawl to the backside of the hill and slide down on his rump.

Below the backside of the hill, a piece of siding from the shed sat on the ground. The piece of siding stood no taller than him, its width, a little wider than the two of them. George, having a great idea, dragged the broken board from the shed to the hill months ago.

He wanted to stand on top of the board and slide down the side of the hill until he reached the water. Even though he couldn't muster the courage, he wanted to hit the water and surf to the other side. He would get the siding positioned at the top, but never pushed off.

Today would be different. It felt different. Today he would do it. He would stand on top of the board and slide down.

He dragged the board from the back of the hill and placed it at the apex. He sat on the board holding his place with his feet on the ground. He knew the drop couldn't be steep, but from his vantage point, it looked like a death drop.

"You're going to f-fall in the w-water and get wet, G-George," Hillary said, pointing at the water. "Then Jenny Gr-Greenteeth will come up and g-grab you."

"I'm not going to fall in," he said confidently. "Now, watch out, I'm coming down."

He stood up, placing his right foot in the middle of the board. Would he do this? Finally, he would feel the wind flow around him. "Look out below," he yelled.

His left foot twisted on a loose rock and accidentally began the dissent. The siding hit a rock protruding from the side of the hill, causing him to lose his balance. He hadn't thought about checking for debris on the hill. He tumbled off the board, rolling toward the creek. He stopped short of the water; the makeshift surfboard hadn't been so lucky. It lay next to him, halfway in the water.

Ego hurt, he sat up, inspecting his arms for cuts. There didn't seem to be any.

"See, you almost f-fell in," Hillary said, laughing. She mimicked what she had seen her brother do, wiggling her body around and falling on the ground.

"I hit something on the way down," George said. He started pulling the siding out of the creek but it seemed to be stuck on something.

His sister laughed while on the ground.

"I could have hurt myself," George said, tugging on the siding. "And you're laughing at me."

"I'm s-sorry," she apologized. "Are you okay?"

"Yeah," George said. "I don't know what I hit."

Hillary examined the hill expecting to find nothing, but she saw a hole about the size of her fist had appeared. "Th-there's a hole."

"What?" George asked.

"Did you p-put the hole in the hill?" she asked.

George tugged one more time and the siding popped out of the creek causing him to fall on his backside. Hillary had not laughed at him because she had become immersed in the discovery of the hole his board created.

He needed to try it one more time because of the loose rock under his foot. Even though the trial run ended up being an accident, he thought he knew what to do.

He dragged the siding up to the base of the hill once again and saw Hillary placing her face against the dirt. "What are you doing?" George asked.

"There's a hole h-here," Hillary said with a muffled voice. She had her face pushed against the hill.

"And you're putting your face next to it?" George asked in a disgusted tone. "Something's going to poke you in your eye."

Hillary removed her face from the hole and said, "It's dark in there."

"The rock I hit must have fallen out of it," he said, pulling the siding up the incline of the hill.

She looked up at her brother who had now successfully pulled the siding to the top. "What is going to p-poke me in my eye?"

"A snake," George commented. "You don't know what's in there."

"L-Look for yourself," Hillary said, moving over.

"If it's dark in there, what am I going to see," George asked, sighing, "a fairy?"

"P-Please?" Hillary asked in a high-pitched voice.

George positioned the board like he had done before and readied himself for the descent. "I'm not going to look in the hole."

Hillary shrugged her shoulders and crossed her arms. She wanted to know what could be hidden in there. She didn't know why this seemed important to know. She just felt the desire to reach in and feel around.

"George," she whined, "I want to know what's in there."

"Why?" he asked.

"I don't know," she said. "Can you get me a s-stick?"

"Fine," he said. He knew she wouldn't stop asking until they checked the hole as she wanted. He lost his concentration on the board and stepped off the ground. The board tipped over the edge and he went with it. He fell to his knees and rode the board to the bottom, passing Hillary with a rush. If she wouldn't have moved to complain about needing a stick he could have slid over her.

This time, the board stopped quickly at the base of the hill by digging into the ground, throwing George forward, over the front. He rolled to the water and fell in with a splash.

Hillary saw George falling forward and watched as he and the board flew past her leg. She uncrossed her arms and ran to her brother. "G-George," she yelled, "are you okay?" She saw her brother stand up in the knee-deep creek, attempting to shake the water from his body. His clothes were suctioned to his skin.

George trudged through the water and stepped onto dry land, one foot remaining in the water. "I think I'm stuck," he said, pulling his leg. Something seemed to be wrapped around his foot.

"W-What's wrong, G-George?" Hillary asked, seeing that he couldn't stand.

"I'm stuck," he said, exasperated. "I can't get my foot out of the water."

"D-Don't l-look in the w-water," Hillary said, running to George. "That's how sh-she gets you." She knew this had to be Jenny Greenteeth. Nana's book had been right. She saw George leaning over to look in the water. "D-Don't d-do it."

George looked back over his shoulder. "Do what? I'm trying to see what my foot is caught on."

"Don't l-look in," Hillary said, grabbing a hand full of rocks. She got as close to the edge of the creek she felt comfortable with and started lobbing rocks at his foot.

"What are you doing?" George asked, frantically dodging the incoming barrage of rocks. "You're going to hit me."

"Sc-Scaring her away," Hillary said, continuing to hurl rocks into the water around George's leg.

"Scaring who away?" George asked again, ducking a misguided rock.

"Jenny Greenteeth!" she yelled.

George lowered his head and sighed. He pulled once again and a rock flew directly at his ankle. He felt the rock hit, but no pain came from it. He yanked one last time and the pressure around his foot released, causing him to fall forward.

"G-Go away!" Hillary yelled at the muddy water.

George shook his head. "Nobody had a hold of me, Hillary. My foot got stuck in mud and grass under the water. See." He lifted his foot to show her the dirty shoe. Algae and black dirt surrounded his foot.

"I s-saved your l-life and you d-don't even care," Hillary said, walking to the steppingstones leading across the creek.

"Where are you going?" George asked. The frustration for his sister's antics could not be hidden.

"To ch-check on our trap," she said angrily. She looked down at the water and carefully took her first step. She spoke to the water in an angry voice. "Don't you e-even think about it."

"What about the hole?" he asked.

"I don't c-care about the hole," she said, hopping onto the other side of the creek. She didn't want to be near the water anymore. Jenny Greenteeth had almost taken her brother. "There's probably nothing in there anyway."

Exasperated, George hopped onto each of the stones, meeting his sister. "It couldn't be Jenny Greenteeth, Hillary."

"You d-don't know that," she responded.

"You're right," he agreed. "I don't know, but I promise my foot got stuck in the mud."

"Did the s-sandwiches get wet?" she asked, pointing to his pocket.

Mrs. Winstock had made them peanut butter sandwiches and put them in a Ziploc bag to keep them fresh. If asked, she would make them sandwiches to take with them when they ventured into the woods. She told them that having a snack available would prevent them from having to stop playing to come back home to eat.

George had placed the bag in his back pocket of his blue jeans which were now soaked. Being too excited to slide down the hill, he had forgotten to take the bag out of his pocket and now they were probably ruined.

George furrowed his eyebrows as he reached into his back pocket. He pulled out the Ziploc bag noticing that water hadn't seeped into it. He relaxed his eyebrows and opened the bag. The smell of peanut butter filled his nose and his stomach growled.

George wiped his dirty hand on his wet pants. He reached in the bag and extracted one of the sandwiches, hoping to be right. He sighed with relief when he saw that no creek water had entered the bag. But some of the peanut butter had been squeezed out of the sandwiches.

"They made it," George said, turning the sandwich over in his hand to show Hillary.

"Can I e-eat it?" Hillary asked. She rubbed her stomach. It growled lightly beneath her hands. "My tummy is rumbling."

George laughed at this. She sounded just like Winnie the Pooh from the stories which had been read to them on a nightly basis by their mother. That great golden bear who talked to Christopher Robin always cheered her up. That silly bear always chased honey and always ran into trouble. George wondered if they were silly 'bears' who were going to run into trouble. *Not likely*, he thought.

George handed the sandwich over to Hillary and then pulled the second sandwich out. He crumbled the bag, placing it in his back pocket, not wanting to leave litter in the woods. He would put the bag in the trash when they got home.

The second sandwich didn't look as good as Hillary's. It looked mangled and smashed beyond recognition. More peanut butter had to be stuck to the inside of the bag than he previously thought. "Mine doesn't look so good."

Hillary ignored him while walking away. Her eagerness to see what they had caught in the trap pulled her back to the clearing. Before getting to the area leading to the clearing, she gobbled her sandwich up.

George walked behind her attempting to eat his sandwich carefully. He didn't want to get the brown gooeyness on his fingers. He failed. It stuck to his index finger as he took his last bite. Not thinking about the dirty water, he had just fallen into, he licked the remnants from his finger. The twisted, messy sandwich tasted just as good as a non-twisted sandwich.

They now stood in front of the path leading to the sticky snare. "Are you ready?"

"Of c-course," she said, placing her hands on her hips.

"Follow me," he said, making his way into the woods.

He led the way through the thick trees, this time holding the branches for his sister. A branch snagged his back pocket and he twisted his body around to remove the grip it had. While twisting, the branch pulled out the plastic bag from his back pocket.

"You l-lost the bag," Hillary said.

"I'll get it when we come back out," George answered. No point going back now. They had to come back in this direction once they realized they hadn't caught anything. They were almost to the cactus.

They passed the cactus, pushed through the last bit of trees, and emerged inside the open, flowery area. Butterflies fluttered above them and a few flies buzzed over their heads. George moved his hands back and forth to get the annoying pests out of his face.

"Where'd they come from?" he asked, looking around at the number of bugs flying in the air.

"I think your tr-trap worked to g-good," Hillary said, looking at the flying insects.

George examined the flowers. The path he created earlier still led to the flower with his sticky snare beneath it. His plan had worked perfectly. "Wait here," he said, starting to walk through his path.

"But I w-want to s-see, too," Hillary complained.

"Hold on," he said. George went a bit faster this time since the path had not disappeared. The sight of the flying insects excited him. His trap might have worked. He knew a fairy wouldn't be in there, but maybe he had caught something else.

Hillary ignored his command and followed quietly behind him. She waited for him to turn and scold her, but the insects flying in all directions seemed to distract him from saying anything.

Hillary became fascinated by the flying creatures around her. She didn't pay attention to George who had stopped at his destination. As George bent over, she bumped into him, causing him to fall forward. Because she looked at the bugs and not at George, she fell with him.

The drop seemed so long, a lot longer than it should have been. The flowers vanished beneath them. Reddish-brown dirt replaced the beautiful flowers they had almost destroyed. George hit first followed by Hillary on top of him.

"What are you doing?" George asked, pushing his sister off of him.

"Nothing," Hillary said. "I w-wanted to see if w-we caught anything."

"Ahh," he growled. Even though the flowers vanished beneath them, he stood up immediately to see if they had ripped them from the ground. There were no flowers. They seemed to have vanished right before his eyes, leaving only reddish-brown dirt under them. A single flower had remained in the center of the dirt. Could this be the flower he hid the sticky snare under?

The perfect circle they stood in was outlined by grayish mushrooms that had popped up out of nowhere. Beyond the ring of mushrooms, the field of flowers had not been disturbed. He could still make out the path beyond the circle of fungus leading back to the woods.

"Is this a fairy ring?" Hillary asked.

"I don't know," George answered, confused. His eyes darted back and forth examining his surroundings. He knew this couldn't have been here before. How did a ring of mushrooms grow so fast? "There's something wrong about this, Hillary."

"Wrong?" she asked. "What c-could be w-wrong? We f-found a fairy ring."

"Let's get out of here," George said, pulling at his sister's arm.

She stood with his help. The sensation of dizziness hit her as everything around them grew extremely fast. The single little flower now towered above them. The mushrooms, which had been around them, were now very far away and extremely tall.

"What happened?" Hillary asked, grabbing her brother's hand.

"I think we just shrank," George said with a shaky voice.

"It just grew from the ground," Hillary said, pointing to the single flower in front of them.

George's flower stood alone in front of them with a pink piece of gum the size of a car surrounding its base.

"Is that-?" Hillary started to ask.

"Yes," George said, interrupting her. He took Hillary's hand and backed away from the gum feeling the danger it posed to them. She did not protest being pulled by her brother. He would have never thought a piece of gum would scare him so much. "That is my sticky snare."

A loud flapping noise echoed in the distance. He could feel Hillary grip his hand tighter. "What is that, George?" she asked in a hushed whisper.

"I don't know," he responded in the same hushed whisper. "But I think we're about to find out."

A butterfly flew over the mushrooms in the distance. Its wings were the color of a strawberry with large black dots. Four other butterflies flew behind it as if in some sort of formation. Each of their wings had been colored orange and blue. They landed in front of the children. Butterflies didn't look so harmless from this point of view. Their faces were black and their wings were large. Coarse black hair protruded down their bodies. Their antenna moved slightly as if searching for something lost in the air.

George backed up again, pulling Hillary behind him. He didn't know what to do. There had been nowhere to run. He felt very vulnerable to be in the open like this.

The butterflies shivered as if they were cold and their bodies morphed into tall thin people. Their wings shrunk down into small dragonfly-like wings. Their heads, which were once bug-like, took on shapes of normal humans. Their eyes were like crystals, sparkling in different colors -- green, blue, and brown. They seemed to be so clear. The bugs' hair grew into long strands of silver hair from which tiny pointy ears protruded.

The front fairy looked older than the four behind him because of his aged skin and his air of authority. He wore elegant robes, the colors of his former wings that shimmered and danced as he moved in the sunlight. His long graceful fingers moved elegantly across his face, rubbing his hairless chin.

73

The four fairies behind him wore beautiful robes the colors of their previous wings. Two were female and two were male. The females' eyes were larger than the males and their full lips were more defined; more colorful. Each of them had their hands behind their backs as if waiting for a command.

Hillary peeked around her brother. "George, I think fairies are real."

"Really?" George asked sarcastically.

"Nana and Mrs. Winstock was right," Hillary exclaimed. "They do exist."

The elder fairy opened his mouth to speak, but only a harmonic soothing voice could be heard. It sounded as if he sang to them.

One of the female fairies placed a hand on the elder's shoulder and joined her voice with his soothing harmonic one.

"Bah," the elder said. His hands flew as if talking with them. The female removed her hand and elegantly placed it behind her back. "I forgot I have to speak in the despicable human language. It's a travesty. Only for the queen will I lower myself to…" he stopped, looking at the children who seemed very confused by his outburst. He straightened himself up and placed his hands by his side. He forced a smile. "The Queen wishes you to visit her."

"The queen?" Hillary asked, coming out from behind her brother.

"Yes, my dear," the elder said, "The Queen, the ruler of our land."

George still did not say a word. He held onto his sister's hand, not wanting her to get too close to the fairies before them. "I wish to go home," George said.

"Home," the elder said, holding his arms out with a smile across his face. "You are here because you wanted to catch us. Did you not?"

George looked at the elder with a curious look. "How do you know I wanted to catch you?"

"My dear boy," the elder said, stepping forward, causing George to take a step back, "I mean you no harm. You placed traps like that," pointing to the gum George had left, "throughout our land to catch us and now you stand before me saying you did not."

"Throughout your land?" George asked. "I put that one trap."

"So you admit it?" the elder said, turning to his four followers, raising his thin eyebrows, and shaking his head. He turned back to the children and placed his hands behind his back while bending slightly toward them. "You see, I am here on the queen's behalf to bring you to her for…let's say a meeting."

"A meeting?" George asked, unsure about a so-called meeting. "My sister and I want to leave. I'll pick my sticky snare up and take it with me. I am sorry."

"I'm not leaving," Hillary said, trying to pull away from her brother. George glared at her.

"Sticky snare you call it?" the elder asked curiously. "That does have a certain ring to it," he raised his voice slightly irritated, "since it is sticky and it most certainly would snare any helpless fairy wandering by."

"I didn't catch any fairy in our trap," George said.

"Oh," said the fairy. "But you did. There are many fairies below Fairy Court right now sickened by your...sticky snare."

"What do you mean sickened?" George asked. "I just placed the sticky snare a few minutes ago."

The elder's eyes grew large. "Liar!" he sang angrily. Hillary once again moved quickly behind George. "You humans think you own the land. I have asked you nicely and I won't ask you again to come with me."

"I think I want to go home now, George," Hillary said whining. "He scares me."

"You haven't seen scary," the elder said motioning to his followers behind him. He sang once again.

George and Hillary were caught off guard as a large net appeared above them, thrown by the followers from behind the elder. They were immediately snagged in the sticky net.

The elder gracefully moved before them. "How do you like *our* sticky snare?"

Hillary screamed. She had started to cry. George pushed against the netting only finding the more he moved, the more he became stuck to the sides.

"Let us out!" George yelled angrily at the elder fairy.

"Soon enough my young, human children," the elder said as a yellowish gas appeared over them.

George covered his face and coughed from the nauseous fumes. His eyes became heavy and he realized what the fumes were. These fairies, which have been talked about for years as good helpers of the woods, are nothing but bad fairies attempting to kidnap him and his sister. He slowly fell into sleep just as he had fallen into the land of fairies.

"Hillary, hold…your…" George forcefully said but had been too late. His sister had already succumbed to the fumes and had fallen into a deep sleep beside him. He too finally gave in to the gas, thinking of that golden bear, Winnie the Pooh. They had found trouble as he had always done, but they didn't have a Christopher Robin to help them out of their mess.

"Nighty, night," said the elder fairy, wiggling his abnormally long fingers at him.

Chapter Five
Fairy Ring

Sam stood at the arched, iron-gate looking beyond the evenly spaced bars to the woods behind it. Moss had grown on half of each of the bars on the antique gate. An oval, metal plate depicting a large oak tree with what looked like sunrays in place of the root system had been welded across three bars.

A silver, tarnished chain ran down the crossbar, held by a fairy atop a brass bell. A brass vine loosely circled the bell from the head to the lip. The clapper had a thinly braided rope attached to it.

Sam gently closed his hand around the braided rope, careful not to tug on it. He pulled it close to him and opened his hand to examine it. The rope reminded him of the many lectures his mother had given him about not entering the woods without ringing the bell first. "It is a courtesy to the woodland creatures," she would say.

He let the rope go and unlatched the gate. He walked through the gate and shut it behind him. Taking a deep breath, he started to walk down the dirt path leading further into the woods.

The woods would not be his much longer. Mr. Drake would own them and would probably build a fence around the land to keep anyone from trespassing. He planned on playing with his children for a little while before dropping the news on them. He wondered if his gesture would anger them more when they found out about the plan to sell the land? Would they take his gesture as a bribe to not be angry at him?

He reconsidered his plan to play first. He needed to tell them the truth. Unfortunately, he would destroy their plans for the day and then spend the rest of the day picking up the pieces he had shattered.

After taking a few steps in, he started to dread the idea of telling them. Why did he have to sell the woods? He could just call Mr. Drake and tell him he had changed his mind, but he knew that wouldn't fix the trees. Keeping this land meant spending more money and time trying to repair something his mother, The Green Thumb, couldn't bring back to life.

"They're in trouble," a female voice whispered in his ear. Sam stopped and spun around, expecting to see someone else standing in the woods with him. Nobody seemed to be around him.

"Hello?" he questioned, leaning into the brush to his left, hoping to see somebody. He started to think the voice had been in his head. No answer came out of the woods.

"They're in trouble," the voice repeated, this time louder.

Sam quickly spun to his left, hoping to catch whoever whispered to him. Could he be losing his mind? Nobody had been in the woods with him, other than his children. Were the kids playing a trick on him? If so, he felt as if he deserved it for what he needed to tell them.

Sam's heart started to beat faster. "Hillary, George!" he yelled into the woods.

They did not answer, they did not laugh. He could only hear the dried leaves scratching together from the slight wind. The woods seemed to shrink around him as he became worried.

A slight movement in his peripheral vision caught movement to his left. His attention quickly honed in on a white butterfly fluttering in and out of the brush line.

"Follow them," the voice said excitedly.

Dead leaves crunched under his feet as Sam walked into the brush line to his left, pushing limbs out of the way. He figured the voice had to be coming from that direction.

"Okay, kiddos," he said raising his voice. "You got me."

Again, no response came. The white butterfly flitting back and forth seemed to be the only living thing in the woods. He followed it foolishly, hoping it would mysteriously direct him to the voice or his kids. He had never seen a white butterfly before and this first encounter appeared a bit too strange. It seemed elusive; popping up in front of him and then disappearing, just too suddenly appear further to his left. It would flutter a bit then disappear, only to reappear to his right.

Sam had walked so far into the woods that he became surprised to see the dying oak tree appear to his right. The brick wall could partially be seen to his left through the trees. The oak's branches spanned outward like an umbrella creating a canopy. Its dying leaves danced slightly from the wind he could not feel. Beams of sunlight cascaded down to the grassless ground, creating a translucent curtain effect.

"What am I doing?" Sam asked himself.

He turned around in the direction he had come wanting to get back to the path. He felt like a distracted dog chasing a butterfly through the woods. He pushed around a slender tree as his foot caught something on the ground and caused him to lose his balance. Grabbing the tree prevented him from falling flat on his face.

"That could have been bad," Sam uttered.

He looked down to see what he almost broke his ankle on. An old wooden structure protruded from the leaves, piled around the base of the slender tree. Sam pushed the leaves away from the structure, revealing a birdhouse. The hole that allowed birds to enter and exit faced toward the tree.

Sam kneeled to examine the weathered box. He touched the top, causing some blue paint to chip off. A thin layer of moss splotched the rotting wood. The birdhouse brought a familiar memory to the surface of his mind. He picked it up and rubbed away some of the moss, revealing a butterfly-winged fairy etched into the wood.

As a child, he watched his mom build this birdhouse. He had watched her nail the thin nails into the wood, forming this box. He had helped her paint it bright blue and they had set it outside to dry in the sun. Once dry, she had created this fairy on the side, carving the image carefully. He remembered the butterfly wings being white with black dots. Those dots were now faded from age. The etched image of the fairy had barely been noticeable due to weathering.

He had asked her where she planned on putting it. She had told him she planned on placing it in the woods, near the brick wall for her little, special friend. They hanged this box on this tree in the woods with a piece of twine. Over time, the twine must have rotted and it fell to its resting place.

Sam smirked at the memory. He knew that every creature in her Fairydom had been her special friend. His mother had stood back after she placed the house. "Rest easy my friend. You now have a home."

Sam hadn't thought anything strange from his mother talking to something he couldn't see. This had been a normal occurrence in his life. She would sit in different locations throughout the woods and just talk. Nobody responded to her. She talked as if she had an invisible friend. Now he realized she probably had gone so deep into her beliefs that she made up creatures to talk to.

The house vibrated gently in his hands as if something inside had run into one of the sides. Could something be living in the birdhouse? Curiously, he peeked inside, careful to not get too close to the hole. He didn't want whatever it could be to jump out and bite him.

The house shook again. Sam took the house away from his face quickly but nothing came out. He pointed the hole of the birdhouse down to the ground and shook it. No mystery creature fell out, only clumps of honeysuckle. The white flowers seemed to be dried out. What would place honeysuckle inside of this old birdhouse?

Once again, Sam brought the hole to his face to see if anything would emerge. Something popped out suddenly and nipped him on the nose. He grabbed his nose, more from surprise than pain, and threw the birdhouse to the ground. It rolled into a bush leaving half of the house exposed.

A hummingbird jumped out of the hole and hopped around the box to look at Sam. He had never seen a hummingbird land on its feet. He would have sworn the little birds didn't have feet due to their nature of flying so fast, zigzagging around flowers. But this one did not fly. It bounced up and down like a boxer in a ring taunting Sam to get closer. It seemed to want to fight.

"Careful, little guy," Sam said. "I think I can take you."

Sam reached for the birdhouse since the little bird no longer inhabited the wooden box. The hummingbird jumped up and pecked Sam's hand as if to tell him to leave everything alone, but yet still didn't fly. Sam noticed, with surprise, that the hummingbird had no wings. Why would this bird be so feisty without wings? Maybe it needed to be this feisty to live.

Sam wanted to return the birdhouse to the area he took it from, so he reached for it a second time. The hummingbird jumped up and pecked his hand again. Sam withdrew his hand and decided to leave the birdhouse where it sat.

"Okay, okay," Sam said, putting his hands up. "You win. I'll leave it alone." He walked backward, not wanting to turn his back on the little harmless bird for some reason. He watched the bird jump up on its house, turn its head in an awkward sideways position, and dive down into its newly relocated structure.

Sam turned back to the path. His kids had to be at the creek playing on the hill. The butterfly suddenly appeared in front of him leading him back to the path. "It may seem like I am following you," Sam said, "but believe me, I'm not." Sam jokingly wondered if the butterfly could be following him.

Now he talked to these bugs. Could he wind up like his mom and start talking to random creatures? Could the bugs have been a mental manifestation that caused her to think that she talked to fairies?

He pushed through the tree line and stepped back onto the path. He walked to the intersection leading either to the dying oak tree to the left or the creek to the right. He could see the hill in the distance, but his children were not playing there. He could see a board lying in front of the hill. He walked toward the creek hoping to see them behind the mound. Could they be hiding from him, hoping to scare him senseless? He mentally prepared himself for the surprise, but it never came.

Sam stopped as he got to the edge of the water and looked around. They had been here. The ground looked wet on the other side of the creek and it appeared that one of them fell into the water.

He knotted his eyebrows together in thought. "Hillary, George!" he yelled again. No answer came. "Where could they have gone?"

Becoming a bit worried, he quickly walked back to the intersection, hoping he missed them at the dying oak tree. But shouldn't they have heard him yell for them? Surely, they weren't that caught up in whatever game they were playing to ignore him.

Movement caught his eye, making him look in that direction. The white butterfly had appeared again in the woods, fluttering its wings casually. A piece of plastic slowly flapped on a branch below the butterfly.

As he stepped forward into the woods, his foot shifted slightly under his weight. He lifted his foot and looked at the sole to his shoe. A piece of dirty pink gum that had to have been tossed onto the ground by his children, stuck to the bottom of his shoe.

"Come on," he said to no one in particular.

He reached out and snapped a twig off the closest tree. He didn't want to give the gum a chance at spread any further on his shoe. It would be hard enough to get it off now. He could imagine how hard it would be to remove if he waited until he got back to the house. He would have a talk with the kids about throwing gum in random places in the woods.

The stick proved to be a good tool to remove the gum. He pushed the stick into the gum and twirled it while scraping down the sole of his shoe. It must have not been chewed very well, because it came off a lot easier than he expected.

After inspecting the bottom of his shoe for any remaining gum, he tossed the stick into the woods. It landed on the opposite side of the trail, just inside the wood line. Making a mental note, he would pick it up later.

Sam stepped into the woods, moving tree branches out of his way. This proved to be more difficult for him to navigate than he thought it would be.

Surely, the Ziploc bag couldn't have belonged to George or Hillary. They knew better than to bring trash into the woods and leave it.

He continued to push through the branches until he finally managed to reach the bag. He opened it, releasing a strong aroma of peanut butter into the air. He rolled the bag up and placed it in his jeans back pocket.

"Kids?" he asked the woods. No response. There had been no indication that they were still out in the woods. Had he missed them leaving the woods when he got sidetracked with the hummingbird? He decided to look further in this wooded area. The bag could have gotten snagged on the tree when they crawled through here.

Cactus lay directly in his path. The oval-shaped pads branched off in different directions. To his surprise, there were two separate bundles separated by a safe dirt path. He walked by being mindful of the thorns on the green pads.

Once again, he pushed through more trees, dodging and weaving through the thick limbs. One final push and he came to an open area covered by a canopy of tree limbs. The area had been filled with yellow flowers with a perfect circle of reddish-brown dirt in the middle. In the center of the reddish-brown dirt grew a lone flower. It seemed as if all the other flowers scattered as far from it as possible.

A ring of mushrooms created a barrier between the dirt and the yellow flowers. Sam wondered if they were trying to keep the other flowers away from the loner in the center. The flowers seemed to be concentrated in the large canopied area, leaving no room to walk. Looking closer, he could see some of the flowers had been pushed aside, carefully. It led to the ring of mushrooms.

To the best of his knowledge, this area had never existed. "What is this?" he asked, leaning down to the flowers. He touched one of the pedals and it seemed to shiver as if tickled.

Curious, Sam walked through the disturbed flowers, being ever so careful to not step on a single one. Could the path have been made by George and Hillary and if so, why?

He kneeled when he arrived at the dirt circle. He touched the caps of the mushrooms amazed by their existence in this formation. Seeing this circle of mushrooms brought back a memory of his mother talking about a similar formation regarding the fairies.

"It's a portal, bridging the land of fairies and humans," his mother had said. "Stepping in the center will whisk you away to their world."

"It can't be," he whispered. Sam laughed at the thought of this being a fairy ring. What if it could be true? What if they existed? A part of him suddenly became excited about this discovery. Another part dreaded the idea. Could it be real? Could his children have fallen prey to this ring and ended up in the land of fairies.

He refused to get caught up in the fairy theory again. George and Hillary must have come over here first, seen the ring, and gone home to tell Mrs. Winstock. He felt foolish in the thought of his children within the land of fairies.

Fairies don't exist. At least that is what he kept telling himself.

Do it, he thought. *Just jump in. What could it hurt?*

How would this work? He prepared himself mentally as if he were jumping into unknown water. He first placed the tip of his shoe onto the dirt. Nothing happened. He placed his foot flat on the dirt half-expecting it to suck him in. Nothing happened. He withdrew his foot.

"Here goes nothing," he said, jumping onto the reddish-brown dirt causing a small plume to erupt under his feet. He steadied his balance with his hands and arms outstretched. When nothing happened again, he lowered his hands in defeat. He knew he must look like a fool.

Part of him wanted to believe this would take him to the land his mother had always talked about. Did he think that chasing these fantasy creatures as a child would turn out to be something as easy as jumping into a ring of mushrooms?

He took a step to the single flower and leaned to look at it. "I wonder what you did to be singled out."

Beneath the flower sat a piece of gum wrapped around the base. Bewildered, he saw the white butterfly gently opening and closing its wings. Had this been the same butterfly that he had been following through the woods?

"George," he said irritated. He reached for the gum. "This thing isn't catching anything but bugs."

He flattened the gum attempting to free the butterfly's appendages. The butterfly fluttered its wings, flying from the trap. It fluttered next to his face, touching it gently. He smiled and thought, *Was that a butterfly kiss for releasing it?*

He watched the butterfly soar upward and then dive down toward him. It fluttered around his head and landed on his shoulder.

"You're welcome," he said laughing. "I will get this trap out of here."

"Thank you," the voice echoed as he started to reach down to retrieve the gum.

Sam stood and twisted his body in shock. Who could have appeared behind him without making a sound? His foot became tangled in something he had not seen. The white butterfly fluttered its wings in front of his face causing him to fall backward. As he fell, the view of the world changed drastically.

He seemed to be falling in slow motion as the mushrooms and flowers seemed to grow rapidly in a blur. Sam realized the motion he felt could not have been him moving in slow motion. He had been shrinking rapidly as the land around him swallowed him up.

The ground quickly stopped his fall. He stood, confused by what had just happened. He looked in amazement at how everything had changed. He froze from the sight, becoming overwhelmed by the sheer implications this had on his existence.

He placed a hand on his mouth in awe as he slowly turned around to take in the sight. Had his mother been right this whole time? Had she been talking to these creatures? A pang of guilt started to well up in him. He thought his mother had been crazy. Then the tantalizing sense of fear took over.

George and Hillary had to have come here. They had to be in this land with the fairies. They could be lost or worse. Snakes, birds, spiders, rats, everything would be so much bigger here.

They must be here, he thought. Their tracks lead right to the ring. The voice thanked him. Who had been talking to him?

He knew the voice had to be that of a fairy. He yelled out, "Where are you? What did you do with my kids?"

A sweet smell distracted him. He knew the smell but could not place a finger on the source.

"They're not here," a soothing female voice spoke in an almost harmonic tone. It had been the same voice in his head, but this time the voice seemed different. It held weight. He turned to the single flower, noticing it now towered over him. The pink gum lay undisturbed at the base of the flower. He identified this as the sweet smell. There were no fairies or any beings' insight.

"What do you mean not here?" Sam yelled. "Where are my children? Are they not in Fairydom?"

He thought back to all the stories he had been told as a child, but every story had been told about nice fairies in the woods. His mother always talked about how the fairies were perfect in every way.

"I don't know what Fairydom is," the voice said. "But they have traveled through the portal and have been taken."

They were here, in this land. This is bad. He had hoped they went to the house to tell Mrs. Winstock that they had found a fairy ring.

"Taken?" Sam asked, shaking his head. Everything seemed to be happening way too fast. "Where have they been taken?" He now became scared and agitated at the voice talking to him.

"I will take you to them," said the voice calmly.

"No!" Sam yelled. "Bring them to me so we can go back through the ring." He didn't know exactly how he could do that, but if he had his children maybe they could figure it out together.

"I can't do that," said the voice. "We have to go to them. The queen has requested to see them."

"Queen?" he asked, looking around to see if he could spot the thing talking to him. "What Queen? I want to see them now."

"The Fairy Queen, Tygira, is the leader of our realm," the voice said. "We must speak to her about releasing your children."

"Releasing?" Sam asked angrily. "Are they prisoners?"

The voice seemed to giggle. "We do not have prisoners. No harm will come to your children. Please allow me to take you to them."

Sam ran his fingers through his hair, frustrated at the thing that spoke to him. After sighing, he said, "Fine. Take me to them."

"I am a fairy," the voice said. "Please do not allow my presence to frighten you."

"I want my children," Sam said aggravated. "I don't care what you look like."

A whooshing sound came from above in short bursts. He looked up and saw what looked like a human flying down with large white butterfly wings attached to its back. He finally saw the being to be that of a woman, a beautiful woman. The woman landed on her feet in front of Sam and her white wings closed behind her, disappearing as they never existed.

She wore a shimmering white gown that sparkled from the sun above. Her eyes were larger than normal human eyes but very clear as if made from blue crystal. Her white hair, looking very thin, had been combed back behind her head and tied off in some sort of bow. Her fingers were a little longer than normal but were very well cared for. A pink substance covered part of her left arm and ran down her leg which protruded from a slit in her gown. This must be a fairy.

Sam backed up, not sure how to feel. She is real. This is real. All these years he had been upset at his mother for talking about them and here is one standing in front of him. "You're a fairy?"

"Yes," she said smiling largely. "And you are human."

Sam slowly nodded his head. He wanted to touch her, to feel her skin. He wanted to prove to himself that she existed. He refrained. He did not want to frighten her.

"As you can see," she said, holding her arm out, "this sweet tasting food seemed to be a trap for us fairies. I can't get it off. The more I touch it the more it sticks to my skin."

Sam immediately recognized the gum. It smelled and looked like the watermelon bubblegum, the same bubblegum George had laid down and called sticky snare. This had also been the same trap that had caught the butterfly.

"Were you the butterfly I rescued?" he asked.

"Yes," she said. "Because you rescued me I brought you here to see your children. You saved my life."

"It's called sticky snare," Sam said, walking closer to her. He couldn't help himself but be amazed by the beautiful fairy before him.

"What?" she asked.

"The trap you were in," Sam said, pointing to the gum under the flower. "It's called gum, but my son calls it sticky snare."

"Oh," she said looking at the stuff on her. "How do I get it off?"

"I don't know," Sam said honestly. Sam reached out to her, but she backed away.

"I'm not going to hurt you," he said.

"I know," she said. "You have a good heart. I can see it in you."

"You can see my heart?" Sam asked covering his chest.

"No," she said. "I can see you are a good human. I do not fear you. I don't want you ending up like this." She touched a piece of the gum attached to her arm and pulled it

93

away. Her hand became covered quickly. Strands of the gum stretched as she pulled her hand away from her arm. She twisted the strands until they tangled around her hand, creating a pink glove.

Sam put his hands to his chin thinking of a solution. It seems the trap worked too well. He thought back to the time when Hillary got gum in her hair. How did his wife get it out? Peanut butter. He just so happened to have a bag with some peanut butter in it. He reached in his back pocket for the bag he had retrieved from the tree. "Where did it go?"

"Where did what go?" the fairy asked blinking her eyes. For some reason, this reminded Sam of shutters on a camera.

"I had a bag with some peanut butter in it," Sam responded. "I seem to have lost it."

"No," the fairy said. "It isn't lost. It's in the flowers over there." She pointed.

Sam started to quickly walk in the direction she had pointed.

"Where are you going?" she asked.

"Follow me," he said. "I think I have the perfect thing for your sticky situation."

She followed him through the building-sized mushroom stalks and into the flower forest. "We don't have anything here for it," she said. "The queen has tried everything."

"Not everything," Sam said stopping. He looked around at the massive flowers. He knew he could easily get lost in this large jungle. "Can you please take me to the bag? It would be a lot easier for you to lead. I might get us lost in here."

"Lost?" the fairy asked. "I don't get lost."

"Good," Sam said. "Can you lead us to the bag?"

"This would be much easier if you had wings," she said, walking past him. He looked at her back, not seeing her wings. They had vanished as if she didn't have any at all.

"It is just up ahead," the fairy said. After a minute of walking, the bag came into view. It lay on the ground stuck between flowers. The mouth of the bag had opened and the smell of the peanut butter floated in the air.

"What is in the bag?" the fairy asked curiously.

"Peanut butter," Sam said. "My wife used peanut butter to get gum out of Hillary's hair a few years ago."

"What is a 'wife'?" she asked.

"My partner, my friend, my companion," Sam said.

"A mate?" she asked again.

"Yes," Sam said, finding the conversation funny.

"Where is she?" she asked, continuing the questioning.

"Gone," Sam said. "She vanished awhile back."

"What is pea butter?" the fairy asked another question. "You said you had some in the bag."

"Peanut butter and yes," he said. "It is hard to explain what it is. It has oil in it to remove the gum."

"What oil?" she asked.

Sam stepped into the open bag, looking inside the clear plastic. It seemed so unusual to be climbing into a Ziploc bag. Who would have ever thought he would fit in one? "You'll see," he said, walking carefully inside.

The bag had a slippery surface as he walked on it. It also seemed a little warmer than he would have expected. The smell of roasted peanuts filled the air. Due to the slipperiness, he decided to crawl. Crawling made it much easier to get further inside. The walls of the bag moved slightly from the wind, he guessed, causing him to fall to his stomach until it stopped. The plastic echoed loudly from the movement, making him think of a cave system. Everything about being small seemed so different. Could crawling in the plastic bag be dangerous? He hadn't even thought of the possible dangers.

He quickly made his way to the back of the bag and scraped peanut butter from the wall. The creamy brown substance felt strange, almost like putty. The aroma appeared to be so much stronger than he had anticipated. Breathing through his mouth seemed to be the best way to deal with it. He turned to leave with the two handfuls. The fairy stood directly behind him, cocking her head to one side.

"What are you going to do with that?" she asked pointing at the substance in his hands.

Sam held out his hand to her. "Can I see your arm please?"

"Yes," she said, showing her arm to him.

"No," he said, "can I please hold your arm? I need to rub this in the gum."

She paused, thinking about the request. "How do I know this will work?"

"Trust me," he said "This will mix with the gum and make it easier to pull off. It will not stick to my hands or any other body part of yours."

She nodded and leaned forward.

He placed the handfuls of the brown goo on her arms smothering the pink gum. "Rub this all over the stickiness like I just did."

Sam reached down to remove more peanut butter. He gave this to the fairy and watched as she methodically smothered the gum with it until no pink gum could no longer be seen. Her arm, hands, and leg were covered in brown.

"Let's get the last of this on your skin," he said, allowing her to scoop what had been left in his hands.

The fairy pulled at the pink substance in amazement as some of the gum came off of her arms. It did not stick as it had before. She pulled at the gum on her legs as it came off in chunks. "You have saved us."

Sam scraped the peanut butter off his hands as best as he could. He needed water to wash it off. He didn't want to smell like peanut butter for the rest of the day. "All you need is water to wash the rest off."

"I can fly to the water," she said excitedly. She ran to the entrance of the plastic bag and leaped out. White wings shot from her back. She opened them wide and fluttered away. Sam crawled out of the bag and started to wipe the remnants of the peanut butter off of his hands onto the ground. Specks of dirt had helped aide him in the removal process.

Sam went back into the bag and found large drops of moisture clinging to the inside of the bag. He reached up, putting his hands in the droplets. As soon as he touched it the water rushed down his arms, allowing him to clean his hands.

He sat on the edge of the bag, looking around in astonishment. He had just saved a real-life fairy, a fairy he had sworn just minutes ago did not exist. When he found his children and left this land he would owe Mrs. Winstock a huge apology.

CHAPTER SIX
HONEY RUN

Listle had been a collector of human objects for many years. His burrow, on the south side of Fairy Court, held all of the precious trinkets that he could manage to carry into the secret hovel. His sister, Thily, and he admired the trinkets, creating stories of how the humans had created them and used them. They had the desire to live among the humans, to be one.

Everything they knew about humans came directly from the assumptions made from the collection. They, like every fairy, weren't allowed to interact with the tall beings that lived in the large box beyond the walls of the realm. This didn't prevent the humans from trying to communicate with them though. Listle had many chances to communicate with them but feared the punishment from doing so.

Just like every fairy, they were attached to groups of plants. Listle and Thily had been attached to a group of flowers called Dorta. The attachment meant they were the caretakers of that group. They provided water and nutrition when asked of them. This rarely happened due to the plants' ability to care for themselves. Nature provided water from the sky and the soil provided nutrients. The fairies were nature's way of having a failsafe if the plants were to fall on hard times. If the plant group died or had been removed, the fairy either joined another group or wandered around until it became absorbed by the land. Not a pretty picture if you were a fairy.

Listle stood among his group of red wildflowers, satisfied with the day's progress. His sister sat on a pebble, looking out into the woods. Her orange hair, which had been separated into three tails, glowed in the morning sunlight. Her tight blue tunic and dark-green, frog skin leggings contrasted with her bright hair.

Listle preferred baggy clothes because he didn't like feeling confined. He felt that his red tunic matched the blonde spiky hair on his head. His brown, baggy pants could hold many objects if he happened to come across something curious. He wore moss-covered shoes on his feet, unlike his sister who preferred to be barefoot.

"Are you seriously going to the bee's nest?" Thily asked Listle over her shoulder.

"Yep," he replied.

"You know they are going to get you sooner or later," Thily said.

"Later, rather than sooner," Listle said smiling. "I need more of that golden sweetness."

Thily picked up a flask attached to Listle's waist. The seed had been hollowed out with a corked top to hold liquid. "You know, if you had a bigger container, you wouldn't have to make so many trips into the hive."

He pulled his hip away from her, pulling the canister out of her hand. "If I had a bigger canister, they would see it and I would definitely get caught."

Listle leaned down to a kneeling position while translucent dragonfly-like wings grew from his back. They moved in a hum, and he lifted from the ground. He zipped right and then left. "Are you coming?"

Thily jumped from the pebble, sprouting her wings, and floated next to her brother. With exasperation, she said, "Let's go."

They circled the big oak tree called Fairy Court. They didn't want to gain the attention of the other fairies. Listle loved the honey within the beehive and didn't want to share it. He wouldn't have shared it with Thily if it weren't for her continual nagging.

Tree limbs with browning leaves zipped past them. The view around them blurred from their speed. They saw the airspace ahead of them and could quickly dodge any objects that appeared before them. The beehive appeared in the distance, perched inside the hollow of an old dark tree.

The tree had died and had been dead as long as they had been alive. The tree had been one of the first trees to die from the Darkness that slowly made its way through the realm. The Darkness had been here for a long time and would eventually consume everything within the woods. All of the fairies knew this to be true but persisted in the endeavor to prevent it from growing any further.

"There it is," Thily said, stopping in mid-air. Her wings beat so fast they seemed invisible. She didn't want to go any further because she feared the bees buzzing around the hive. "Good luck."

101

Listle had a talent for sneaking around the hive without being detected. He had done this many times before. She would watch him fly to the hive and disappear into the trees. A little while later he would pop out of thin air, holding the canister full of honey. He had always been smug about it while sharing the honey with her. He never revealed the secret to her and she never asked how he had done it. She didn't want to know because she never cared to get that close to it. Even though some of the bees were fairies, they didn't like any outsiders in the hive.

"Be back shortly," he said, tapping on the canister with his finger. He flew upward into the trees and vanished from sight.

Thily flew to a nearby branch and landed on it. She kneeled, watching the hive for trouble. She didn't expect any. Listle had been good at this.

She sat on the branch a lot longer than normal. What could be taking him so long? Normally he would be back before she realized he had left. She started to get worried as she paced back and forth on the tree limb. She knew her brother better than anyone and she knew he had to be in trouble. She could feel it in her wings.

The buzzing from the hive grew exponentially. She looked over to the hive and saw bees pouring out. They flew in unorganized formations. Had the bees caught him after all?

"Get out of here!" she heard Listle yell at her in a panic. He flew above her, flying away from the formations of bees.

She did what he said without question. She dived from the limb, opening her wings to catch air, and saw many bees closing in on Listle. She flew to the ground to avoid being seen. Listle would eventually fly far enough away from them and they would give up their quest to capture him.

****

Listle flew recklessly through tree branches, attempting to get away from the bees that pursued him. He needed to get some distance between them. He had yelled at Thily to fly away, and he hoped she had listened. The bees meant business.

Thily, of course, would poke fun at him for getting chased. She had told him they would catch him, but these bees weren't chasing him for the honey. He had taken something of value from the hive, something which didn't belong there. It seemed to be of value to the yellow and black bees. Luckily, he placed it in a pouch hanging around his neck.

His crystal yellow eyes scanned the area around him attentively for bees. He couldn't see any, so he shot behind a large tree leaf, using it as a barrier to hide. The bees were fast and angry, proving to be a good combination for them.

While continuing to look for the bees, he felt for the seed flask attached to his hip. It held honey, the sweet nectar of the bees. He had gone into a chamber that he had never been in before. A tubular honeycomb had been built in the center of the room. After scooping honey into the flask, he reattached it to his waist. He went to the honeycomb and a light appeared through the paper-like material. It seemed suspended in Royal Jelly, the bee queen's special honey. After puncturing a hole in the side of the honeycomb, he reached in and plucked the

103

object from the draining yellow liquid. He needed to be careful not to touch any of the queen's honey due to its nature of solidifying quickly on any body part it touches. He had stowed the shiny object in a pouch around his neck so he could examine it closer at a later time.

Getting a break, he decided to continue his flight. He needed to get far enough from the beehive so the bees wouldn't follow him. Once he had flown the necessary distance, he would be able to enjoy the sweet taste of the honey in his flask.

Cautiously, he leaped from leaf to leaf, looking for the flying bees. A buzzing caught his attention and he ducked down, anxious that he had been caught. Poking his head up from a leaf, he noticed the stillness and silence of the air.

He could see Fairy Court. To get there, he needed to make it past a few more trees. The bees shouldn't follow him that far away from the hive. They definitely wouldn't go to Fairy Court. The fairies and the bees had a complicated relationship.

Just as he bent to leap from the branch, he heard a voice whisper in his ear.

"I told you so," Thily said.

Listle jumped away from Thily as if she were a spider getting ready to eat him. He looked back at her. She had placed her balled-up fist on her waist and glared at him with her honey-colored eyes. She had that I-told-you-so look on her face.

"Are you crazy?" he asked through clenched teeth.

Thily turned and sat on a small knot poking out of the tree. She patted into the air toward Listle, trying to quiet her brother while laughing at his excitement. "I couldn't help it."

"Those bees could have heard me if I yelled properly," Listle said, adjusting his tunic. "What are you doing here? You're supposed to be near Fairy Court to meet me."

"You were taking too long, as always," Thily sighed. "I thought I would come to see if they got you like I said they would. I told you those bees don't like intruders in their hive, but nooooooo, you wouldn't listen to me."

"Look," Listle said, leaning into his sister. "I have the honey. They didn't get me."

"Let me see," she said eagerly, holding her hand out.

"I also have something in here," he said, holding up the pouch.

"What did you take?" Thily asked, poking at it. "It's too small to be a larva."

"I don't know what it is," Listle said, releasing the pouch, allowing it to fall to his chest. "We'll have to examine it when we get into a safer area."

"You don't know what you took?" she asked, shaking her head. "That could be anything."

"It has never been there before," he said. "Whatever this is, it's amazing."

"Yeah," she said. "I hope it is worth what you got yourself into."

"I have a feeling this is worth everything."

Thily loved Listle's collection of human trinkets, but going through this much trouble for an amazing treasure seemed quite ridiculous. She had been curious to see the contents of the pouch, but not enough to ask now. She wanted the contents of the flask Listle held around his waist.

"Can I get some honey?" she asked, reaching into a pocket of her tunic. She withdrew a hollowed-out black seed that had been corked.

"Not now," Listle said, looking around.

"Come on," she said, pushing the seed to him. "Those bees aren't going to find us. They probably already went back to their hive."

Listle hoped that to be true, but he needed to be extra cautious. Whatever object he took might make the bees more apt to follow him longer than usual. He cupped his hands over his ears, attempting to hear the bees buzzing around. There were no sounds around them that would identify it as a bee. Had they given up their chase that easily? Could the object he took be of any value to them?

He pulled the flask away from his hip and opened the cork. Thily removed her cork and eagerly watched Listle pour the thick golden ooze from his seed into hers. She placed two hands on the seed and smiled. She couldn't wait to taste the delicious liquid.

After pouring a good portion for her, he corked his seed. Thily did the same and put hers away into the hidden pocket. Listle released it, letting it fall to his waist.

"Now, can I see your treasure?" she asked.

"Let's wait until we get back to Fairy Court," he said, still not believing the bees had fully given up the chase. "I don't want to pull it out and lose it."

"I guess you're right," Thily agreed. "But I don't think those bees are around here anymore."

"Better to be safe than sorry," he said.

"Do you have a plan to get there safely?" Thily asked.

"Why do we have to make a plan?" Listle asked. Thily always seemed so cautious. She always needed a plan. Listle saw himself as a free spirit. He didn't need plans. He would just do what he wanted and deal with the consequences when they arose.

Thily stood from the knot. She tapped her chin with an index finger. "If the bees are out there, they will be after you."

"Yeah," Listle said, attempting to amuse her.

"If you give me your honey, I will fly to Fairy Court," she said. "You fly off in the opposite direction with nothing. If they are out there, they will chase you down. The honey will be safe."

"One problem," Listle said. "I have this thing in my pouch."

"Why are they going to chase you for that?" she asked. "You know all they care about is their honey. That would be the only reason they would be chasing you."

"Look," Listle argued. "We fly off together. If they come, we split up. Easily done. No plan needed."

Thily appeared to be visibly agitated. "Listle, the bees will get you. You never listen to me. Why do I try so hard to help you out?"

"Because, I'm your brother," he said. "And you like to be in charge."

"Well," she said, pointing a finger skyward. "I did warn you about going into the hive so often. I told you they would eventually catch you."

"You are a part of this too," he said. "You like the honey I get. Next time, I won't even share with you."

Thily dropped her finger from the air. "Fine. We will fly blindly to Fairy Court, but at the first sign of those bees, I am out of there. You are on your own."

"I'll beat you," he said, falling from the tree branch and sprouting his wings. He lifted quickly from the drag. As he lifted higher into the air, he saw them. Three bees were hovering between him and Fairy Court. They were blocking his path. He stopped, not sure if they had seen him. They had.

He did not have time to look around for Thily. He shot upward into the sky and the bees gave chase once again. How did they find him? Were they just waiting for him to appear? They flew faster this time, catching up to him. He had to find somewhere to hide.

He scanned the area and saw a spiny bush. He knew the spines were thick, and he felt he could get inside without the bees being able to. He breathed heavily, trying not to panic. What would they do if they caught him?

No fairy he knew had ever been in the beehive. Being the only one that he knew, he wanted this secret to stay a secret. His visitations had always been brief. He never went too deep in the hive, fearing he would be caught. He knew a queen lived in the center. Why had he gone so close to her?

Today, he ventured too far into the hive and found the object. He didn't tell Thily any of this because she would just nag him about taking too many chances. Taking chances had always been the best part of the adventure. Maybe he had gone too far this time. If he would have gone to his normal spot, he would already be back in their secret hovel, enjoying the sweet golden liquid of the bees.

The bees were directly behind him, getting closer by the second. He flew over the spiny bush and dived straight down, pulling in his wings at the last second. Landing on a small branch afforded him a quick view into the thorny bush. He looked for an opening in the thorns, hoping he could get protection from the bees.

Spotting a narrow gap between two thorns, he extended his wings and jumped graciously from the branch. His wings allowed him a slower, calculated decent between the thorns. As soon as his feet crossed the barrier, he drew in his wings.

His feet landed on the bushes gnarled limbs that had grown together over time. The spines had twisted together, creating a cave-like dome. It reminded him of being underground, like his hovel. Cracks lined the bottom part of the domed structure. Sunlight had only been able to penetrate the gap he had fallen through. He hoped the thorns on this bush would protect him from the onslaught of his pursuers.

If they found him in this thorny cave, he would be trapped. The only way out seemed to be through the same hole he came in. The small cracks allowed him a view of the ground below. He wondered if he could break some of this weathered plant to escape if the bees came at him through the hole. This had now turned into a waiting game.

If Thily knew he had been trapped, would she get help from other fairies? If so, his secret might be revealed and he would have to explain why and how he had gone into the hive. Would Queen Tygira punish him? Would she give him over to the bees as punishment? The idea of the bees using their stingers on him made him cringe.

Listle sat down in the center of the self-made prison, peering through the hole. Bees started to arrive above the bush. Had he been spotted? Did they know where he could be hiding? He wanted to start the escape now, but he didn't want to bring attention to himself by making a lot of noise.

He watched in glee as each of the bees buzzed off in the direction of the hive. He had won. The object is his and he would hide it in the hovel. The need to look at it overwhelmed him, making him reach for the pouch.

Something large hit the side of the dome, causing him to fall over. The bees weren't done with him yet. Would it be too late to break the floor and make an escape? They would see him crawl out and nab him. Another hit, to the top of the dome, shook decaying plant matter all around him. Cracks started to form around the thorny enclosure.

Listle realized that the plant had been dead a long time, a victim of the darkness that plagued the land. If the bees continued this barrage, he would be done for. They would take him and the object back to the hive to be put in front of the bee queen.

The bees were being a lot more aggressive than they had ever been. Listle braced himself on the blackened thorns, fearing the bees would be inside in a matter of time. Knowing his time would be short, he took the flask from his waist. He would enjoy drinking this honey right in front of them. Would this be an insult? Yes, yes it would. He would enjoy the golden sticky liquid before they did whatever bees did to fairies that entered their hive and stole from them.

A whistle came from outside of the thorny dome. "Follow me! I have your honey!" he heard Thily yell.

Listle stood, looking out through the opening in the spines. Hovering in mid-air, Thily held her seed out to the bees. She attempted to lure the bees away from his prison. If it worked, he would be able to escape. He had a feeling it wouldn't work. The bees were not after the honey. They wanted what he had in the pouch.

He watched as three bees moved away from the thorny dome. They slowly moved in Thily's direction. Could her distraction be working? Were they going to her? She hovered backward slowly while shaking the seed. "Come on!"

His chance finally came. He jumped up to the hole, grabbing the top. As he started to pull his way out, the bees stopped their advance on Thily and turned to him. Listle had just pulled half of his body out when a bee smashed into the spines next to him. He fell to the bottom of his prison, sprawling onto the floor.

These bees were more aggressive about his capture than he previously thought. He didn't know what else to do. He now knew there wouldn't be any chance for him to get out of this. He pulled the pouch out of his tunic and opened it.

A loud, crashing sound to his left caused him to turn. The object fell from his pouch. He grabbed it, securing it in his hand. He ignored the bee that had managed to become stuck in the wall, slowly making its way into the dome.

Listle held a translucent, oblong crystal in his hands. A cloudy blue glow came from within it, his favorite color. He ran his finger across the top and watched the solid rock ripple from within. This feature excited him. Nothing he had ever found made him giddy with excitement as much as this crystal. The rippling seemed tranquil, making him forget about the carnage taking place around him.

A loud crash drew his attention away from the crystal, bring him out of his relaxed state of mind. The bee had finally made its way into the death trap. It stood on top of the brown decayed plant it had just crushed. Fear no longer coursed through him as a second, larger bee broke through the wall of the dead plant.

Listle held the stone with two hands, pushing it out in front of him. "Is this what you want?"

The bees paused. They watched Listle closely. Listle moved the stone to his left, they followed it. They weren't moving a lot, but it appeared to be enough to tell that the bees were definitely after the crystal he had stolen. He moved it to his right and they followed.

"Drop it!" a voice came from below him. Thily had yelled at him as she watched this encounter beneath the thorny dome.

Listle looked at the stone. He didn't want to drop it. It drew him in, intoxicatingly. He knew this treasure had been the most beautiful thing he had ever found and he didn't want to part with it. "I can't."

"They want it, Listle," she said. "I don't think they are going to let you out of there."

Listle cradled it in his hands. "I can't let it go."

Listle stepped back and tripped. Thily had maneuvered her hand through the spines and grabbed Listle's ankle. Listle fell back, releasing his precious treasure. He watched in horror as the crystal tumbled from his hands to a hole big enough to fit through. He lunged for it and missed. The crystal had fallen taking a piece of Listle with it, at least that's how he felt. Looking through the hole, he watched it bounce off a leaf and then vanish into the woods below.

The bees buzzed to life and flew out of his prison, leaving Listle alone and unharmed. They flew quickly, down to the ground where his crystal lay somewhere on the ground of the woodlands. They had vanished just as quickly as his precious find.

"Are you okay?" Thily asked. She looked down at him from the hole he had come in through.

"Yeah," he said disappointedly, standing up. Dusting himself off, he said, "I lost the crystal. Something tripped me and I dropped it."

"I did it," Thily said. "I grabbed your foot."

"Why?" he asked, flying up to her. He sounded tired. "Why would you do that?"

"The bees were going to hurt you," she said. "They weren't after the honey. They wanted you. Once I saw the crystal and saw how they reacted to it, I didn't have a choice. I saved you."

He felt disappointed. He flew upward to Thily. "Thank you. I just couldn't drop it. It seemed so beautiful."

Thily patted her brother's back. "Well, at least the bees are gone. We have the honey and the bees have what they want."

"The crystal is special," he said, holding his hands out like he still had it in his hands.

"Did it sing?"

"Sing?" Listle asked, looking at her with confusion. "No. It had the appearance of water in stone, but you couldn't feel the water. It just seemed so strange."

"But what made it so special that the bees would chase you this long?" Thily asked.

"I don't know," Listle said. "But I would love to find out."

"No," Thily said, waving her hands at him. "No more of your adventures. Every time we go on one, we end up in some kind of trouble. Remember the time you went looking for that crystal you said looked so beautiful? It turned out to be a frog's egg that gleamed in the sunlight."

"Yes," Listle said smiling. "I almost got eaten by that huge bullfrog."

"I did get eaten," Thily said quivering.

"No you didn't," Listle said. "That old bullfrog spit you out."

"Only because I had the egg," Thily argued. "Trust me; you don't want to feel a frog's tongue around your body."

"Seriously, this had been the most beautiful crystal ever," he said, cupping his hands again. "You would touch it and ripples seemed to wash over it, but it stayed solid."

"No," Thily said again, flying toward Fairy Court.

"Come on," Listle responded, flying after her. "We will just give them a little while to calm down and then I will go get it back. You don't have to do anything."

"I don't want anything to do with it," she said.

"Yes, you do," Listle said. "You just don't want to admit it. You have fun doing stuff like this."

"No," she said. "I don't like having fun like that. Do you think it's fun watching you get chased by those bees? I couldn't do anything to help you."

****

Fairy Court stood tall amongst the thinner, less majestic trees. Its canopy of limbs towered over the area. Dried brown leaves covered the woodland floor. At one time green, lively grass flowed at the base. At the bottom of the tree, there were large arched doors that led to the internal court.

Listle and Thily stopped flying when they saw Queen Tygira, queen of the fairies, standing outside the doors. Her elegant green robe glittered in the sunrays shining from above. Her long blonde hair flowed gently in the breeze. She stood with her arms crossed in front of her, impatiently.

"What's going on at Fairy Court?" Thily asked. "Does she know about the bees?"

"I have no idea," Listle responded. He knew the queen rarely made an appearance outside of Fairy Court. She seemed to be waiting for something or someone. It couldn't have been him. It had only been honey and a crystal. Yes, it had been a pretty crystal, but he didn't think it could be so important for the queen to be involved.

Horns within Fairy Court blew loudly. These are the Calling Horns. These horns notified fairies in the lands to attend court if they wished to. When the Darkness first invaded their land, every fairy would attend court to hear the progress to finding a cure. Over many years, a cure had not been found and attendance to court fell. Today, fairies poured into the arched doors bowing to the queen, who ignored them.

"May I ask why you are outside of the borders of Fairy Court?" a voice said behind Listle and Thily. They turned, startled by the voice.

An older, thin fairy, Asroth, hovered behind them. His wings beat fast. Asroth happened to be the queen's advisor and head guard. Behind him were four other Guards of Fairy Court. The four guards each held lines that lead to a net made from spider silk. Inside the net were two sleeping fairies.

"Are we supposed to be near Fairy Court?" Thily asked, slightly peeking around Asroth to the net. Did she know the two mischievous fairies? "Nobody told us."

"Where have you been?" Asroth asked, following her head with his.

"Here and there," Listle said, pointing in different directions. He too peeked around Asroth. He flew to the side and attempted to move closer to the net.

Asroth quickly intercepted him. "You should have been at Fairy Court," Asroth said, pointing to the tall tree with his long fingers. "Queen Tygira commanded that all fairies of the realm come to Fairy Court and await further instructions. There have been many fairies caught in the pink human trap."

"Pink human trap?" Thily asked.

"Yes," Asroth answered. "The trap is called sticky snare. It is sweet and it is sticky."

Sticky snare, Listle thought, *what a curious name*. Now, Listle wanted to go find some. It couldn't have been as good as honey. By the sound of it, the sticky snare sounded a little dangerous.

"We didn't get those instructions," Listle said. They would have been told to stay close to Fairy Court if they had been at their group this morning. He didn't want to tell him where they had been due to the questions that would be asked. They would have to tell too many lies to keep their secret. He hated lying. Tell the truth seemed so much easier because the truth never came back to bite you in the rear. "We were with Dorta this morning. Our group doesn't seem to be doing so well."

"The humans have been trying to get rid of us for millennia," Asroth said. "It seems they finally created a trap to do this. If you know what is best for yourselves, I would suggest your staying away from it and staying in the Fairy Court grounds."

Listle and Thily both nodded. Thily wanted to know more about the humans who had supposedly made a trap to catch fairies. Could this be the humans from the boxed structure outside of their realm?

"Make your way to Fairy Court," Asroth commanded.

Asroth passed Listle and Thily in the air. The group of four guards followed behind slowly. Thily watched the net as they passed. The fairies inside didn't look like fairies at all. They were wearing strange clothes. Their ears were not long and pointed like a fairy's ear.

Beyond the captured whatever-they-were, Listle saw the queen turn and walk through the Fairy Court doors. He now knew she hadn't been looking at them. She had been waiting on Asroth and the guards.

"Listle," she said, tapping him on the shoulder. He had been staring at Fairy Court.

Listle looked at her. "Thily, the queen went back into Fairy Court. She had been waiting for them, not us."

"Well, that's good," she said. She grabbed Listle by his loose tunic. "The two fairies in the net are not fairies, they're human."

"Human?" Listle asked, pulling away from her. "They can't be human. Humans can't get here."

"But their ears were short and round," she said, touching her long pointy ears.

"Have you gone mad?" Listle asked her. "Humans cannot come to our land."

"I bet those are human children," Thily argued. "Their clothes are strange too."

"And?" he asked, shrugging his shoulders.

"Listle," Thily yelled. "Did you not hear what he just said about humans?"

"Yeah," he said.

"The two in the net did not look like any fairies I have ever seen," she said.

Listle turned his head, looking at her. "There is no way those two are human."

Thily removed the seed from within her tunic. She tugged on the top until the lid popped off. "What if the humans have figured a way into our world?" she asked taking a swig of the sweet nectar.

"What happened to you?" Listle asked.

"What do you mean?" Thily asked.

"You want to do something, don't you?"

She looked at Fairy Court. She had never wanted to create an adventure. She had always been too busy cleaning up the messes Listle had gotten them into. "I want to know who they were."

"Why?" he asked taking the cork off of his flask. He took a quick sip enjoying the taste of the spoils. Oh, it tasted so sweet and pure.

"I don't know," she said. "What harm would it do if we go and take a peek?"

"You want to go take a peek?" he asked. "Then what?"

"Then nothing," she said. "Mystery solved."

"You don't know the first thing about adventures," he said. "First, you find a reason to go on the adventure. You then jump in and let the adventure take you away. You don't just start one and then nothing. This seems to be boring."

Thily thought about what he said. Had he always done this? Had he pondered the idea of an adventure and jumped in? If Listle had always done this, she always jumped in with him and suffered because of it.

"Okay," she said. "What if we rescue them?"

"What?" Listle asked. "No. The queen would be furious. You don't go looking for trouble when it involves the queen."

"I am not an adventurer," she said. "I just want to know who they are."

How could he make this less boring? He needed a reason other than just seeing and leaving once he got his answer.

What if they were human? He had been thinking about this all wrong. If they were human, they would have human things. He could take a human object and add it to his collection. He had been good at taking things without being caught, most of the time.

"Fine," he said. "We go and see who they are. Not much of an adventure."

"Listle, we are only going to look."

"I know," he said. He wouldn't tell her that he planned on taking something from them. He needed to keep that part secret. She didn't need to know anyway.

CHAPTER SEVEN
FLIT

Sam's mind raced with different emotions. Fear encapsulated the majority of his thoughts. His children were kidnapped in a world of unknown creatures and unknown dangers. He could not imagine how they could be feeling at this moment.

Were they scared? They had to be. They couldn't have expected to find a fairy that would whisk them off to Fairydom. Wanting to go to Fairydom had been different than actually coming to Fairydom.

If it weren't for the fear he felt for his children, he might have felt a little excited to have stumbled into a world which he didn't believe existed. Stumbled isn't the right word. He had been brought to this world by a fairy with butterfly wings who wanted to help him find his children.

Being here turned out to be surreal. He tried to remember discussions Mrs. Winstock and his mother had about the inhabitants of this land. All of those memories seemed so foggy to him. Why couldn't he remember all of the details? He couldn't remember because he refused to believe in fairies and had flushed all of the knowledge of the little ones out of his mind due to it being rubbish.

Sam rubbed his head in frustration at the amount of time it had taken the fairy to remove the gum from her body. Where could that blasted, beautiful fairy be? He looked in the air, using his hand as a visor from the sun. She had to be here soon.

"Think," Sam said to himself, standing up. He paced back and forth, keeping an eye on the sky and the surrounding terrain. He knew there could be something very bad behind the tall mushrooms and he didn't want to be surprised.

A memory flashed in his mind. "The queen is the ruler of the land," his mother had told him. "She is a radiant being with the wings of a large butterfly while all other fairies have wings as you would see on a dragonfly."

How did his mom and Mrs. Winstock know so much about this land? Were they guessing as they delved deeper into the lore and just so happen to get things right? Could this fairy be the queen of fairies? Could she be lying about where his children were? So many questions swirled through his mind. None of them could be answered until she returned.

"Is she the queen?" Sam asked himself. Her wings weren't as vibrant as he would think a queen would have.

In the distance, he could hear happy laughter and knew it had to be the butterfly-winged fairy. From her reaction, he knew the peanut butter had worked.

"It worked!" the fairy's voice sung above him. She glided gracefully down toward Sam, batting her large wings. Her white wings had started to fill with vibrant colors. "You have saved us all, Sam."

Sam heard the fairy sing his name but could not believe it. She knew his name and he had not told her. "How do you know my name?"

123

The fairy landed gracefully before Sam, causing him to back up out of caution. Her wings shortened then retracted behind her. She smiled brightly with her full pink lips. She spun, opening her arms wide as if dancing to music.

"You are a great human," she said happily.

Sam caught himself preparing for an attack and tried to relax. Could the fairy be capable of attacking him? She seemed so happy.

"I am not going to harm you, Sam," the fairy said, smiling brightly. "You have saved me from getting the trap all over my wings."

"How do you know my name?" Sam asked again.

"Every fairy in this land knows your name," she said. "You are the spawn of a great and caring human, Lana."

"My mother?" Sam asked. "How do you know her?"

"She is the creator of our sanctuary," she replied. "I have watched her on many occasions as she came here, attempting to restore life to Fairy Court. She tried very hard at that feat. But I haven't seen her in a very long time."

"Fairy Court?" Sam asked. "This is the place where all fairies gather? Is this also where George and Hillary are at?"

"Yes, to both questions," Flit said amazed. "How do you know of Fairy Court?"

"My mother had been a bit of a know-it-all on the world of fairies," he said sadly. Unfortunately, his mother could no longer speak of the fairies. A feeling of regret boiled in him. How much time could he have spent with his mother talking about the fairies? His stubbornness kept him away from the discussions and he wished that he could have got that time back.

"How is your mother?" she asked.

Sam lowered his head in sadness. "She is no longer with us."

"She hasn't ever been with us," the fairy said, curiously looking behind Sam.

"No," Sam said, waving his hands at her. The next words out of his mouth choked him up. "She died about a week ago."

"Oh no," she said, holding her long slender fingers up to her mouth. "That is not good. Queen Tygira will be horrified to hear this."

"You aren't the queen?" Sam asked, waiting to see how she would answer the question. He learned how to tell when George or Hillary lied to him based on body reactions. George would look up in the air quickly as if the answer to a question were hidden on the ceiling. Hillary would tap her nose or rub her hands together.

"I'm not the queen," the fairy said, tilting her head to the left. "I am Flit. I am only a servant to the queen."

"A servant?" Sam asked.

"Yes," she responded. "I hope this does not present a problem. I can get you to Fairy Court so you can plead your case for your children's release. If you fail, you and I could be punished. I had been concerned that she would do this without speaking to us, but you have the cure for this sticky snare. She would be most grateful for your help. She could come here and take the cure from the bag."

"There isn't enough in there to do much, but I know where to get much more," Sam said, pointing to the plastic bag.

"Then we have struck a deal?" Flit asked.

"If the deal is, I get my children back and you get the cure? Then, yes," Sam said.

"This is good news, Sam," Flit exclaimed. "When we get to Fairy Court, you must stay hidden. If you are seen before I can introduce you, we could both be in danger, along with your children."

"If you could be in danger for bringing me here, then why do it?" Sam asked.

"I have never been disloyal before," Flit said. "I fear what might happen if your children are blamed for their involvement with the traps."

"My children didn't place traps across Fairydom," he argued.

"The queen believes they did," Flit argued back. "It doesn't matter what you or I say about the matter."

"How do we get there?" Sam asked. "I don't think you can carry me to Fairy Court."

"On a normal day, I could carry you," Flit responded. "The trap has affected my flying skills a bit. Lift your arms slightly. I am going to try and carry you from behind."

Sam did as she requested, still feeling a bit tense about the situation. Flit walked behind him and put her arms under his.

She tightened her grip around his chest as the air started to circulate in large bursts around Sam's body.

Ten feet into the air, Flit lost her momentum and dropped back to the ground, slowly.

"Do we walk then?" Sam asked, turning to Flit.

"It would take too long to get there," she said, looking around. "We're going to need some help."

"From who?" he asked, looking with her.

"I have my ways," Flit said.

Flit raised her hands to the tall flowers and a breeze went forth, causing them to sway back and forth. The flowers followed in a rhythmic dance around them until they suddenly stopped. A large, greenish head poked out from behind a flower with a white underbelly. The scales on the head looked like hundreds of large shields placed in a geometric pattern to protect the beast.

Sam focused in on the head trying to see what this could be. The eyes of the beast had large black pupils. "Snake!" Sam yelled, walking backward from it. "Flit, run!"

"No," she said, placing a comforting hand on Sam's shoulder. "This is Slithery, a harmless grass snake. He is here to help us get to your children."

The grass snake moved forward with such ease. Even as it reached Flit, the snake's body remained hidden within the forest of flowers. Sam watched the snake cautiously, but yet with intrigue. From his height, he could appreciate how the snake could move without having legs. It seemed to glide on the ground.

Slithery moved his head close to Flit's face. It stuck out its red slender tongue, wiggled it, and pulled it back in. A low audible hiss exited the snake's mouth, forming words barely recognizable. "Issss thisssss a human you have brought into our land?" The snake turned its scaly head to Sam, looking at him intently with its mesmerizing gaze.

The snake talked? It didn't exactly talk, but it did have speech. Sam felt confused. Did all animals talk? All of this had to be a dream, like the one of his wife turning into a dragon and falling into darkness.

"This is Sam, and yes, he is human," Flit said. "We need to get to Fairy Court, immediately."

Flit waited as the snake stuck out his tongue. Another low hiss formed words. "Why have you done thisssssss? Humansssss are vile creaturessssss."

"Slithery," Flit said. "I have brought him here to help us with our problem. The queen already has two other human children in her care. We need a ride to meet up with them."

Sam moved toward the snake. He is going to talk to a snake as if it were an intelligent being. It spoke, so, yes, it appeared that he needed to persuade a snake to help them. "I assure you-"

Slithery snapped its head to Sam with a quickness he had not expected. Sam fell to the ground, raising his arms in defense as Slithery opened its mouth, discharging a loud hiss. He watched as the small teeth lining its mouth got closer to him. His tongue wiggled in the air, inches from Sam's face.

Then it suddenly stopped. Flit jumped in front of the snake opening her wings wide. "You will not harm him."

"I did not plan on harming him," the snake whispered. "Thisssss human ssssseemssss different."

Sam knew he seemed different. He is smaller and had become less of a threat to the large reptile.

Slithery bowed his head to Sam. "I will help you. I am humbled to be a part of your legacy SSSSSSam. Pleassssse forgive me."

Sam stood from the ground and dusted himself off. He watched Slithery remain still with his head bowed. He looked at Flit with a look of confusion on her face.

"It's okay, Slithery," Sam said, just as confused as Flit. He now found himself consoling a snake who had wanted to attack and possibly eat him? This day has been strange and he knew he hadn't even seen the strangest part of it yet.

"I will allow you to ride upon my back," Slithery hissed. "Your queen will not be happy with you."

Your queen? Sam thought. So the fairy queen isn't Slithery's queen. The queen rules fairies and not other creatures in the land? Could the queen not be as powerful as he thought.

"She is your queen too," Flit said.

"No," Slithery said. "She is not my queen. There is only one true queen."

"True queen?" Sam asked.

"Queen Tygira is the queen of fairies," Flit said angrily.

"For now," Slithery hissed, lying on the ground. He seemed to allow his body to flatten.

"What is going on here?" Sam asked. Mrs. Winstock and his mom talked about fairies as if they were nice. There haven't been any troubles in Fairydom that he could recall. He wondered what they would think if they knew the truth. Fairydom is not as bright and cheerful as they made it out to be. "What is my family walking into?"

"You're not walking into anything," Flit said, glaring at Slithery. "Some of the creatures in this land aren't happy with Queen Tygira because the Darkness has grown faster this last year."

"What darkness?" Sam asked.

"Our land has been dying for many years," she said, pointing out to the woods. "A long time ago, before Queen Tygira ruled our land, another queen ruled. Her name had been Pasny. According to stories, she released a plague within Fairy Court and it started spreading. Queen Tygira toppled her and forced her out of the realm. She left without curing the plague. The Darkness has been spreading ever since."

"Is that why the trees are dying?" Sam asked, rubbing his face, stunned. He couldn't believe what he had just heard. A fairy queen released the plague his mother and he had tried fixing. It would explain why his mother could never fix the problem. This seemed so far beyond anything she or he could fix. They weren't fairies.

"Yes," Flit said. "Your mother attempted to cure something which she could not. Fairy magic cannot even cure it. For years, Queen Tygira had fairies work on a cure, but they could not figure out how. Over time, the ones who attempted to cure the plague became infected themselves. I only know this because of fairy gossip."

"Did they die?" Sam asked.

"Yes," Flit answered, bowing her head.

"Now this gum is causing worse damage to the fairies," Sam said, shaking his head. "I understand why your queen is so upset, but my kids had no idea this would happen."

"I know," Flit said, placing a hand on Sam's shoulder. "That is why you are here, Sam. I need you to talk to her. You have the cure for this sticky snare."

"I will help," he said, reaching his hand to his shoulder and placing it on top of hers. "We need to get to Fairy Court."

Sam looked at Slithery and wondered why the snake had not spoken. The green snake just lay there, silently waiting to be their taxi ride to Fairy Court. Sam expected the snake to interrupt Flit with his objection of Queen Tygira, but it didn't speak out.

Slithery looked at Sam and tilted his head. "If you were expecting me to talk, then don't," Slithery said, hissing the words out of its mouth. "I have sssssaid my piece."

Flit rubbed Slithery's head. "I am sorry, Slithery. You are a good snake. Thank you for helping us."

Flit jumped in the air, extending her wide wings. They fluttered gently as she mounted Slithery's back and then pulled her wings behind her back, allowing them to vanish. She reached her hand out to Sam. "Come on up."

Sam would have to ride on the back of a snake. This snake would take them across the woods to a large tree called

Fairy Court, where the queen of fairies had his children. This seemed so much like a fairy tale and he appeared to be trapped in the middle of it.

Sam took Flit's hand and crawled up, sitting behind her. He didn't know what he could use to stabilize himself on top of the snake. He didn't feel right about holding Flit for balance. He barely knew her and he didn't want to upset her.

"Hold onto my waist, Sam," she said, reaching behind her and pulling his hands to her waist. "This is going to be fast."

He grabbed her waist and leaned forward. She smelled like a fresh flower with a hint of peanut butter. He breathed in her scent and relaxed.

Slithery jolted forward causing Sam to lose his balance. He grasped Flit's waist tighter and then wrapped his arms around her midsection. He knew snakes were fast, but this seemed unreal. The speed that the snake possessed surprised him. Flit's hair flew backward tickling his face. He moved his head back and forth not wanting to let her go. Her hair finally moved enough to allow Sam to see the blurred surroundings.

He looked around the woods, at the blurring green surroundings. The blur turned brown and then green again. Trees and bushes were flying by. The snake slithered across the ground with such grace and speed. At this pace, he knew they would be at the tree shortly.

What would he say to the queen of fairies? Please let my children go? He knew he would have to apologize for them. That is what fathers did when their children messed up. He never expected to have to apologize to a fairy queen for them. What type of etiquette would be necessary for this situation?

He pictured himself kneeling before the queen and kissing her fingers as they did on the television. He would ask her to please let his children go and then she would yell out 'Off with his head!'. That is a grueling thought. He hoped it didn't come to her yelling the statement he read in Alice and Wonderland.

Horns blew ahead of them. They were trumpets of some kind. "They are starting," Flit yelled over the gushing air flowing past them.

The wind slowed as Slithery's pace slowed. The snake moved to the left, allowing Sam to see the large tree they had tried so hard to revive. Brown dirt, which used to be green grass, surrounded the base of the oak tree. High up in the branches, from what he could see, were barren, lifeless twigs. They seemed to hang off the tree in a depressed state without the bright green foliage.

Flying beings could be seen darting back and forth. He knew they had to be fairies. Small holes had been drilled into the tree in random places. Each hole exuded a light from within.

Slithery stopped under the formation of small rocks outside of the parameter of the dirt. Flit dismounted Slithery, nimbly flying upward. She held her hands downward toward Sam.

"You know what happened last time you tried lifting me in the air," Sam said, reluctantly interlocking his hands in hers.

"This time we will not be flying up," she said, lifting him in the air slowly. She maneuvered to the left and fluttered to the ground, allowing Sam to plant his feet safely on the dirt.

Flit fluttered toward Slithery and landed on the ground next to the snake's head, patting it. Sam shook slightly from the thought of the snake eating Flit where she stood. What prevented it from eating her or him?

"Thank you, Slithery," Flit said.

"It isssss my pleasssssssure," Slithery hissed, moving away from them.

Sam waved and then slowly stopped. Why would he wave to a snake? It couldn't wave back.

Flit looked at him curiously. "Did you want Slithery to come back? Did you forget something?"

"No," Sam said. "I…never mind. What do we do now?" he asked.

"I will go into Fairy Court to see if it's safe," she said. "I need to ensure you will not be noticed before I introduce you. I also need to see if she has your children with her. It would be devastating for you to come along and be spotted if she hadn't spoken about why she has brought them here. Once you are introduced, you may approach the queen and explain everything. Then you and your children should be able to go home on the promise of returning with the cure."

Sam shook his head at her naivety. He had a bad feeling that wouldn't be happening. He hoped it happened, but he knew her plan had been too easy. He knew he had to be prepared for the worse possible scenario. He would be captured along with his children and kept here. What would Mrs. Winstock do? Would she look for them? He knew she would never find them. After all, they were in Fairydom. She would never look here. Why would she? Who would think to look for a smaller version of them?

"You think she is just going to give up my children so we can go home?" he asked.

"Why would she not?" she asked. "You have the cure for what your children were brought here for. She will be happy."

"Okay," Sam said, hoping for the best.

"Stay hidden," she said, flying to Fairy Court. "I will be back to get you,"

Sam sighed in frustration. His children were in that huge tree. He desired to run in the tree and yell out for his children, but he knew it would cause more harm than good. He rubbed his hands together to keep calm while waiting for Flit to return.

Chapter Eight
Queen Tygira

Listle and Thily flew toward Fairy Court in anticipation of their new adventure. Thily thought this adventure would be easy, a quick in-and-out job. Get in, find the fairies, or whatever they were, and then sneak back out, without being detected. Easy fleazy. But there, nestled in the back of her mind, had been that nagging feeling that this wouldn't go as easy as she hoped. Listle would be involved. Listle seemed to make things more complicated than they needed to be, for the sake of adventure.

Fairy Court is the tree and the tree is Fairy Court. It is sacred to all of Fae. Even though Fairy Court didn't look majestic now, it is the tallest and oldest of all trees in the woodland. Before the Darkness came, Fairy Court had been a canopy of green leaves engulfing the entirety of the woodlands in beauty.

At the midpoint sat an entrance to the queen's hall. These halls led to the inner workings of Fairy Court. Royal guards walked the hallways just in case intruders desired entrance. This had never been a problem. Nothing of significance had ever happened in Fairy Court other than boring speeches about how the land had become more engulfed by the Darkness. And these speeches were no more informative than a fairy standing by itself babbling in some unknown language.

Normally, a fairy would enter the tree from the bottom, work their way up a large spiraling stairway to the top of the court, and then enter the hallway leading to the chambers. Flying had been forbidden in the stairwell and Listle didn't want to be seen as they entered Fairy Court. Plus, where would the fun be in walking up a spiraling staircase to look in a room? That would be too easy.

Listle knew it would be faster and much more interesting to gain entrance to the chambers from outside. Flying up the side of Fairy Court seemed more dangerous and he lived for the danger. He desired to make this worthless trip worth the hassle. He wanted to get this over as quick as he could so he could focus on getting back to the beehive. He wanted that mysterious crystal back.

It would be more dangerous to fly up the tree at such a large height due to birds, but birds normally stayed their distance from Fairy Court. Some had been seen in the past. Fairies knew the distance to travel and they were reaching that danger zone. You didn't want to be the fairy regarded in memory as bird food because he went too high.

"Stay close to the court," Listle told Thily as they flew upward. He could see the entrance right above them. "If you spot a bird please let me know."

"Bird?" Thily asked timidly. She had been so focused on finding out who had been trapped in the nets, she had not realized they needed to fly so high. She gazed down to the ground below her and froze. She grabbed the bark of the tree

137

and nervously scanned the air around her. "You didn't tell me we were going this high."

"You are the one wanting an adventure," he said, hovering behind her while smiling. "You know I like an adventure. What if we get chased by birds? Bees and birds in one day. Now, this would be one exciting day."

"I didn't want to get eaten by birds!" she yelled franticly. "A frog is one thing. Birds are completely different."

"Look around," he whispered into her ear. "Do you see any birds?"

She closed her eyes, not wanting to see if she would be gobbled up by a feathered behemoth. Those sneaky birds were known to hide in branches and fly down unexpectedly to catch their prey. Their eyesight is better than great. It is true that fairies too had good eyesight, but becoming bird food made her quiver in fear.

"Thily, we are closer than you think," Listle said, shaking his head.

"How close?" Thily asked, looking up in the direction of her brother's voice. He stood in a doorway smiling down at her.

"This close," he said, disappearing into the tree.

Thily heard him laugh at her expense. His laugh got fainter the further he went into the hallway. She let go of the bark and flew into the hole. "Not funny," she said to Listle who leaned against the wall with his arms crossed.

"Oh," he said. "You should have seen yourself. Definitely worth it."

"I prefer not to think about it," she said, walking past him. She gave him a quick playful shove. "Now where do you think they took them?"

Voices echoed further down the corridor, around a curve. Light magically illuminated the corridor from nowhere but everywhere at the same time. The twosome peered around the curved wall and saw the net holding the supposed humans disappear into a room. The two beings were now in a location Listle and Thily could get to, no searching required.

"Looks like we won't have to search for them after all," Listle said, pointing. There goes some of the fun of this adventure. "We just have to get the guards away from the door long enough for one of us to sneak in to take a look."

"Let me guess who will be getting the guards' attention," Thily said, sighing loudly.

"You know, I am better at sneaking around," he said with a smirk slowly crossing his face.

"But this had been my idea," she whined. "I want to see the humans."

"They're not humans," he said indignantly. "The queen bringing humans into our land is insanity. Humans don't belong here. Plus, how would she bring them here anyway?"

"The bridge," Thily said, without thinking. Of course, it had been the bridge.

"The what?" Listle questioned her.

"The bridge," she said with trepidation. She watched Listle's face contort as if deep in thought. Uh oh. She knew that look. She then quickly said, "It's supposed to be away in and out of their world."

"How do you know about that?" Listle asked. This sounded like something he would investigate later. Why hadn't he heard of this bridge before? He thought he knew about all of the strange things in this land. Surely, Thily didn't know about a bridge to the human world.

"It is something I heard a long time ago," she said. "The older fairies were talking about it one day when I attended Fairy Court. They were whispering back and forth about how Queen Pasny had been forced to leave through the bridge by Queen Tygira. They said Queen Pasny is the one who cursed the land or something like that. The Darkness came from her or so they said."

"Why haven't you told me any of this," Listle asked with his arms crossed. It seemed as if she had held this information back from him on purpose. "I mean, a portal between our two worlds is something big. Could you imagine walking among humans?"

"That is the reason I didn't tell you about it," Thily answered, pointing at him. "You would have wanted to seek it out and try to go to their world."

"Yes," he said confidently. "You know how I feel about that. Can you imagine all of the treasures I could add to my collection?"

"Collection?" she asked. "It would be too dangerous. I think it would be more dangerous than trying to steal the crystal from the bees."

The memory of the crystal he held just a short time ago crept back in his mind. How would he get the crystal back? The bees would surely hide it better next time. He knew they weren't expecting a fairy to just walk in and find it. This time he would need to look for it.

"Never mind the bridge," Thily waved her hands. "What do I need to do?"

"We are going to discuss this bridge when we are done here," Listle answered.

For the sake of identifying the creatures in the net, she nodded her head. "Fine. What do I need to do right now?"

"Be yourself," Listle said. "Go to the door and tell them something about the queen that will get them jumping."

"So you want me to lie to them?" she said smartly. "You want me to lie to the guards? Tell them the queen requires their assistance?"

"Yep," he said shaking his head. "Then run from the door."

"Run?" she asked.

"If you run, they will follow you," Listle said. "When you make it around the corner, duck behind something. Become one with the tree."

"Become one with the tree?" she asked, becoming very confused at the very notion of having to become one with the tree. "What does that even mean?"

"It means vanish," Listle said. "Just hide. They will run past you and you can come back here to see what they have. I will already be in there investigating."

"If I get caught, Asroth will have my head," she said.

"What is he going to do?" he asked. "All he is going to do is blow hot air and throw us out. Trust me, he's a big thorny bush on the outside, but once you get past the thorns he is a squishy fruit in your hand."

Thily shook her head as she walked away. *Thorns still poke you and can draw life force*, she thought. She wondered if seeing what they captured would be worth all of this sneaking around.

Listle watched Thily go into the door and shout, "The queen requires your assistance! Please hurry!" She then ran out of the door, disappearing around the corner, deeper into the corridor. She heard the commotion behind her as the guards followed hastily behind her.

Listle knew it would work. He knew too well how the minds of the guards worked. He once wanted to be one, but the idea of standing guard in one spot didn't sit right with him. He needed to be on the move, searching for the next greatest adventure, pulling Thily into the middle of it.

He ran swiftly to the door and peered into the darkened room. He stopped in his tracks at the sight before him. The room had been lit by greenish lights on sticks poking out of the ceiling. These lights were from lighting bugs. This isn't right. No fairy could extract the fluid from the bugs and use it. This is wrong.

Two figures were seen lying in the center of the room on a feather from a bird. He stepped into the room, wanting to get a closer look at them. He had been wrong and Thily had been right the whole time. How did humans get into their land? The bridge is real. It had to be.

Two human children, a boy, and a girl lay sleeping with the spider net now fully open, laying over the feather. Their ears were not pointed and their clothes were not fairy garb. He knew he had come across something he should not be seeing. He turned quickly, wanting to leave. A figure stood in the doorway, preventing him from leaving.

"Hello, Listle," Asroth said in a hushed, almost sinister voice.

"I didn't take anything," Listle said. "I had looked for the exit and found these two in here."

"It's okay," Asroth said. "Come with me and I will help you out."

Listle reluctantly stepped toward him. He didn't see any other option except to run for the window on the far side of the room. He knew he didn't have the time to pull the curtain back and fly out of here. For some reason, he felt like he needed to run, but there had been nowhere to go. He saw a large smile across Asroth's face. "Why did you bring humans here?"

"Never mind the humans," Asroth said with an almost satisfied tone. He stepped aside, allowing Listle to walk by. "We have a few things to discuss with you and your sister."

"Thily?" he asked. "Did she make it up here, too?"

"Yes," he said. "She is with the queen right now."

"The queen?" Listle asked. He had been caught, and the queen wanted to meet with him. This adventure is turning out to be a little more than he bargained for.

Asroth grabbed Listle's arm and shoved him down the corridor. "We are going to go see the queen right now."

Listle pulled away from Asroth but knew he couldn't get too far. He didn't know exactly what they had been caught doing, other than finding two human children sleeping in a room, a room that shouldn't have existed. The fluid from the lightning bugs should not have been used in that manner.

Asroth guided Listle to the queen's chambers and stepped through the double door. Listle didn't want to do this, but Thily waited there, either to be rescued or to be joined by him. He knew they were cooked. They couldn't escape. He hoped he had been right about Asroth being a mushy fruit.

****

Horns blew, causing George to open his eyes from the forced nap. Thinking it had been his bed, he sat up and rubbed the sleep from his eyes. As he focused, the vision of the room became clear.

The bed he laid upon had the color of grey with white streaks. He knew it couldn't be a bed because he could feel spaces between sections of soft slats. The realization hit him as the memory of fairies forcefully came to the forefront of his memory. He jumped up, hurriedly looking around for the one who had sprayed the mist into his face. There were no fairies in the room.

The small room looked dark with a green glow emanating from four sticks placed in holes around the ceiling, opposite from one another. A window covered in purple cloth glowed a purplish hue.

His sister came here with him. Where could she be? He couldn't see her. "Hillary," George whispered.

"Shhhh," he heard Hillary say from the other side of the room. "They won't let us out."

"Who?" George asked.

"The guards outside," she said, pointing to a doorway leading out into the unknown. Two fairies stood with their backs to them. Their slender wings shimmered in the greenish glow of the room.

"Where are we?" George asked, walking to his sister.

"I don't know where we are, but it's high in the air," Hillary said, pointing toward the window.

George walked to the window and pushed the purple cloth out of the way. Light shot through the opening and lit the entire room. A large feather lay in the center of the room. He had been lying on a feather when he woke up. By the size of it, he knew he didn't want to meet the owner.

George looked out of the window and saw that Hillary had not exaggerated. They were very high up. The ground seemed fuzzy. He tried to focus on the ground and noticed the brownish color of the dirt. He could make out the creek flowing straight ahead. He could see the brown scraggly bushes he always disliked standing across the creek.

"I think we are waiting for the queen to talk to us," Hillary said.

"The queen?" George asked.

"I heard the guards talking about the queen," she said, joining George at the window. "She wants to talk to us about something."

"The sticky snare," George sighed. "She wants to punish us for using sticky snare to capture fairies. We should have never tried to catch one, Hillary."

"Us?" Hillary asked. "I didn't have anything to do with that. I remember you having that idea."

"My idea?" George said, pointing at himself. "But you helped."

"I am the little sister," she said, sticking her tongue out at George. "I have to do what you say."

"Yes," he said, walking to her, "but you never do."

"The queen isn't going to punish us," Hillary said with her hands on her hips.

George looked at his sister confused. He had just noticed his sister had not stuttered. "Hillary."

"What?" she asked, lowering her hands. "Why are you looking at me like that?"

"Why aren't you stuttering?" George asked. "You always stutter."

"I didn't know that I stopped stuttering," Hillary said, finally realizing she hadn't stuttered one time since she had been in this world. "I don't know."

"Is it because we are in Fairydom?" he asked.

"George, I'm not stuttering," she said happily.

George smiled at her while patting her shoulder. "Hillary, we are going to have to find a way out of here. We have to get back home."

"I know," she said, lowering her head. "Why did they put us to sleep?"

"I don't know," he said. The fairy world is completely different than he thought it would have been. His Nana and Mrs. Winstock always talked as if the fairies were nice and cheerful. All they had seen so far were mean and angry beings with wings.

Yes, they probably had a right to be angry at them for putting gum down as a trap, but he didn't think one piece of gum could have made them this angry. Plus, they hadn't even caught a single fairy in it. It seemed like the only thing they caught with the gum were themselves.

George paced across the darkened room. He tapped his chin with his finger. "What would dad do?"

"It's going to be okay, George," Hillary said, causing George to stop in his tracks while she wrapped her arms around him.

"What if she never lets us go?" he asked.

"She is the queen, George," Hillary said, letting him go. "Nana always said the queen is good and nice."

"I will have to explain everything to her and offer an apology," George said, rubbing his head.

"I don't think any fairies were hurt with the gum you put down," Hillary said, walking to the guarded door. "Remember, you didn't catch anything."

George smiled. "If no fairy had been hurt or caught, then why are we here?"

Hillary reached out to touch a fairy wing on one of the guards. George grabbed her hand. "Don't do that."

"I just wanted to touch one," she said. "They are real, George."

"I know," he said, pulling his little sister back to the middle of the room. "You were right. They do exist."

"My friends will be so happy that I have seen a fairy," Hillary said, clapping her hands.

"We can't tell any of our friends," George said harshly.

"Why not?" she asked sadly.

"Because, no one will believe us," he said, looking out of the window again.

Outside of the guarded doorway, a loud bang caused George to jump. Footsteps echoed softly then became louder as someone walked toward their guarded room. "Begone," said a female voice angrily. "I will see them now".

George pointed at Hillary and whispered. "Stay here." She nodded slowly, agreeing with him.

He slowly walked to the unguarded door, trying to see who could be walking into the room. Darkness prevented his eyes from seeing anything. As he reached the door, a tall slender fairy walked in, causing George to step back.

Hillary sighed loudly. George stared at her. This fairy had radiant beauty. Her large, bright-green eyes looked intently at them. Her gown shinned silver with black beads encrusted in the fabric. She held a brownish-green staff of twisted vines. The base thumped loudly on the ground as she let it slide through her loose grasp. Her hand gripped the top tightly and angled the top of the staff toward George.

The top of the staff glimmered from the gems encrusted in it. It seemed yellow but with the greenish lighting in this room, the color could be off. "You're finally awake, I see. I wanted to be the first to welcome you to my land."

"Who are you?" George asked.

"I think she's the queen," Hillary answered him.

"You are correct, little one," the queen responded. "I am the Queen of Fairies."

"We don't want to be here," George said, pulling his sister behind him.

The queen smirked nonchalantly with her bright red lips. "On the contrary, my dear, you tried to capture us. So you being here should be a blessing for you."

"It is," Hillary said from behind George.

"And what is your name?" the queen asked, tilting her head to look behind George.

Hillary pushed George's hand out of the way. She wanted to see the queen. "I'm Hillary," she said, bowing down to the queen in an odd manner. Her legs bent at the knees and her head lowered. Her hands went to the ground, touching it gently, and then she rose.

The Queen tilted her head. "How sweet," the queen said, with a bit of disdain, pulling her staff back to her body. She released the staff into her arm and clapped her hands together in an elegant slow-paced clap. After the third clap, she clasped her hands together as if praying. "How have you come to learn the correct introduction for the Queen of Fae?"

"My nanny, Mrs. Winstock, has told us everything about fairies," Hillary said. "She taught us about the different types of fairies and how they live. George didn't learn because he didn't believe you were real."

George nudged Hillary to stop talking while smiling nervously.

"Is that so?" the queen asked, staring intently at George. "Well, George, we are real and I am real. Do you wish to touch my hand to see for yourself?" She pushed a hand out for George to touch.

"No ma'am," George said politely. The queen pulled her hand back and grasped her staff once again. He glared at Hillary. "I see this world is real, along with the fairies."

"This nanny," the queen said, questioning Hillary, "is who?"

"She watches us while our dad goes to work," Hillary explained. "She always talks about fairies."

"Interesting," the queen said, rubbing her chin. "She must be a wise human to know about us."

"She is," Hillary said happily.

"Well, Hillary, of the human world," the queen gestured a bow back to her without touching the ground. "I am Tygira,

Queen of the Woodland Fairies. I am the ruler of this land and the fairies that live within it."

"Why are we here?" George asked.

Queen Tygira glanced at George. "You are here because you have injured many of my kind. They have become prey to the pink traps you set."

"Sticky snare," Hillary said. "He named it sticky snare."

George tugged on his little sister's shirt to get her to come back to his side.

"Are you proud of the idea that has come to hurt some of the fairies in this land?"

"No," George exclaimed. "I didn't mean to hurt anything. I just wanted to prove to Hillary you didn't exist. I didn't realize this would happen."

"But it did, George," Queen Tygira said. "You are here to tell me how you created this so I can find a way to cure the ones injured from it."

"How could so many fairies be hurt by just one piece of gum?" George asked Queen Tygira.

"One trap?" Tygira laughed. "Are you telling me you only know of one trap?"

"Yes," George said.

"There are many traps placed around this land." the queen said, sounding a bit disappointed.

Hillary looked at George with a curious look in her eye. "We only put one trap down."

"You might know of only one trap," the queen said. "But we have counted twelve so far. My trusted guards are out looking for any others placed in hidden areas."

"George," Hillary said, hurtfully. "What have you done?"

George looked stunned at Hillary. "I didn't do anything. I put that one down with you and that's it."

Queen Tygira smiled. "We know you only placed one trap. The other traps were placed by a human female, one of the old ones. Since you are the creator of the trap, we had just figured that you knew of them."

George wondered who would have placed more of the sticky snare traps out in the woods. The only older female living in the house is Mrs. Winstock. Could she have placed the sticky snare traps down without his knowledge? Why would she want to capture fairies?

"Mrs. Winstock could have been the only person," George said.

"Mrs. Winstock?" Hillary asked.

"So you know of this?" the queen asked.

"No," George said. "I didn't know she planned on placing the traps down last night."

"Why would Mrs. Winstock place gum in the woods?" Hillary asked.

"I don't know," George answered. His mind swam with confusion.

Queen Tygira looked at George for an uncomfortable amount of time and then smiled. "I believe you, George, and if you trust me we can get you out of this mess."

"What mess?" George asked. "You are the queen. Can't you just let us go back home?"

"I am sorry, George," the queen said. "I can't let you go just yet. All of the fairies in the land are angered by this attack on our land. Someone must pay the price."

George looked horrified at this. "What price do *I* have to pay? I didn't do anything wrong."

The queen spun on her heels and shut the doors behind her. She placed her staff against the doors and turned back to the children. "Can I be honest with you, two?"

Hillary and George looked at each other surprised by her question. Could this be a trick? "Yes," they both said at the same time.

"The land is dying. The trees and plants are all dying. We call it the Darkness and we do not have a cure for this disease. This disease had been a curse placed upon our land by a fairy named Pasny. She had once been the Queen of Fairies, but I stopped her from destroying this land and banished her through the mushroom portal you came through.

"This sticky snare business is the best thing that could have happened now. It is bringing fairies together and forgetting about the land dying around them. I don't believe you wanted to hurt any of us, but they do. And they need to believe that for now. I promise you, George, your punishment will be light and easily managed and then you will be escorted back to the portal and you will be able to go home."

"What will my punishment be?" George asked.

"All you have to do is help me," the queen said. "We are having court in a little bit. The fairies in the court need to believe that I captured you to help us. The fairies below Fairy Court are ill and they need more than your help to save them. I will convince them to let you go free."

George wondered how the fairies below the Fairy Court had become ill from a trap of gum. He needed to take the fall for all of the gum placed around the land and they could go home. It sounded like a good idea. At least he wouldn't be sentenced to life in this land. He didn't think his dad would be too happy about that. He knew if they were not home today, they would be in trouble. The police would probably be called and he didn't want to put his father through the agonizing feeling of dread that had come when his mother had vanished.

"I think it's a good idea," Hillary said.

"Fine," he said. "What do I have to do?"

The queen smiled brightly as she removed the staff from the door. "Just act the part and you will be going home."

She thumped the staff on the floor twice. Three guards in green fairy garb opened the doors and walked through the door. They grabbed George by his arms.

"Let me go!" George yelled, trying to escape their grasp. A green vine wrapped tightly around him to hold him in place. "I didn't do anything wrong."

"Don't hurt him," Hillary said, being pushed out of the way.

George's mouth had been muffled with what seemed like a sponge of some type. He tried to wiggle his head away from it, but the fairies were more determined.

"He will be fine," the queen said. "We just need him to be calm while we have our gathering. If it comes to it, he will have his chance to speak to the fairies. You and I need to get to the throne room so we can make our grand entrance."

The guards dragged George out of the room and down a long corridor to the right. Hillary walked beside him and looked at the queen with a glare. Could this be part of the act she had talked about? This seemed too real. Maybe that is the point?

The corridor hooked around to a larger room. This room held a large throne carved from wood. Small circles were deeply etched into the wood along with swirls and lines. They all seemed to form a pattern of wind and water. The dark brown color of the throne made it look very old.

The queen sat on the throne. "Come here, Hillary," Queen Tygira commanded, pointing to an empty spot next to her. "You can sit here with me while we go down to Fairy Court."

Another vine, extending out from a hole in the ceiling, reached out to George and wrapped around him, removing the temporary vine. It lifted him from the ground, suspending him in the air. George tried desperately to get out of the vine that bound him. He hoped this had been part of the act she wanted him to play.

"Asroth," the queen commanded to the guard closest to her. George recognized the fairy as their captor. "Find Flit and ask her to prepare a feast in my chamber for our guests. This is a day worth celebrating."

"Yes, your highness," Asroth said, sprouting his wings from his back. He flew down the corridor to some unknown location.

Another horn echoed from the depths of the tree. A large door opened below the throne, expelling light from the lower depths into the chamber. The throne seemed to hover in mid-air as if by magic. A roaring sound from all the fairies below rushed upward, sending a shiver down Hillary's back. The throne then started to lower into the massive court below. The thought of seeing all of the fairies gathered in one setting made her excited. She looked up at George and gave him a nervous thumb up.

"Here we go dear," Tygira said, sitting back on her throne, chin up, as confident as could be. "This will be a day-long remembered in our realm."

Chapter Nine
Teatherwilly

Horns bellowed a melody from Fairy Court that only a fairy could hear, a custom that hailed from the old kingdom across the great waters. The horns, carved from balsa wood, announced to all fairies in the kingdom that court would begin shortly.

Some fairies would be flying in the direction of the old tree to see why the horns called out to them. These fairies continued to have hope, hope to hear good news regarding the Darkness. Others ignored the calling because they were tired of being reminded that the land had been dying around them, so they continued to do what fairies commonly did. One fairy, in particular, rushed forward, hoping to arrive at Fairy Court before the queen's throne lowered into the great hollow of Fairy Court.

He is Teatherwilly, a member of the Tree Fairies. His long, thin body resembled a tree twig. His four appendages looked like branches from a tree, giving him the ability to hide in plain sight if the need arose. His bark-colored wings flapped expeditiously as he flew to Fairy Court.

Teatherwilly did not like to attend Fairy Court. He is one of many fairies that did not like to hear the queen spout on about the Darkness's progression. He despised Queen Tygira; not because she had been bad to any of the fairies, but because she could not be the true queen. She did not possess the wings of a queen. This unorthodox method of rulership left a sour taste in his mouth.

Today proved that she did not know what she could be doing as ruler of their land. Today is a day that he is ashamed to be called a fairy. How dare she bring humans into their world. Because of this, their world could be threatened more than what the Darkness could ever do. Humans were vile beasts who fought amongst each other for the rights of land, land that the fairies had cultivated for thousands and thousands of years.

Queen Pasny would have never allowed this to happen. She had been strong and would have circumvented the tragedy that the sticky traps had brought down upon them, but she would have never brought humans into their world to see that they were punished for something they were simply unaware of. This could be a deadly game that could get out of hand. He didn't want to think what would happen if word got back to Sam, the children's father, or Lana, the old, female human he trusted due to her caring nature.

He reminisced back to the days before the darkness, before Queen Tygira. Fairy Court had been uprooted by humans and transported to the location where it stands now. She helped migrate the lost fairies further into the woods. Even though most of the fairies had joined her, others decided to remain at the old location. Queen Pasny and he tried convincing the ones who refused to migrate away from the old location, but they denied her request.

He watched Queen Pasny torture herself for many years over the methods she could have used to make them leave the old land. Ten years after they migrated into the new land is when Queen Pasny realized what befell the ones who stayed back. Their wings had fallen off, and they had become unknown servants to the humans who had built their dwelling on the old location of Fairy Court. They now called themselves Lawn Fairies.

Today, the decedents of those same humans were brought into the realm by force. When he heard that Queen Tygira had brought them into their land, he felt a duty to Queen Pasny to go stand in Fairy Court and voice his objection. He knew that his voice alone would not make Queen Tygira listen to reason, but other fairies might hear him and stand with him, at least he hoped they would.

How he wished he had half of the fortitude that Queen Pasny had. He missed his dear friend and wished that she would not have left the realm. She had been accused of causing the Darkness and knew that she felt something this dire had to be her fault, whether she started it or not. Tygira made it known that Queen Pasny had been at fault for allowing such an atrocity to happen. Tygira then motioned for Queen Pasny to be ostracized from the land, other fairies agreed.

Teatherwilly knew Queen Pasny had spent much of her time in fascination over the humans, who had built their house over the old land. She had frequently visited the house, curious as to why they had come here. As far as Teatherwilly knew, she had never learned the answer.

Tygira and Queen Pasny visited the Lawn Fairies. Tygira reported that Queen Pasny only wanted to hold the meeting to get closer to the humans, but he knew that could not be the case; she had already been visiting them. He had been told by Queen Pasny that the visit would be more of a meeting to reconcile the two lands, to help heal their relationship. While at the meeting, the king of the Lawn Fairies had fallen ill from the Darkness. Rumors circulated that Queen Pasny had infected him. She locked herself in her throne room for many days, fearing that she had caused this infection.

Around this time is when the infection appeared in the woodlands. Queen Pasny attempted to cure the land when she first noticed it but kept it secret. Holding this information secret had been her downfall. Fairies on the north side of the woods reported strange black markings had appeared on all of the trees. In a matter of days, the northern woods had become diseased enough to push the fairies from the area. The land's soil had become infected and it grew at a furious speed.

Tygira prompted a vote to rid the land of Queen Pasny due to her involvement in the atrocity. A majority of the Woodland Fairies agreed and Teatherwilly stood by helplessly as they barged into the throne room and took the queen to the bridge between the two worlds. Queen Pasny looked beaten that day. The time in the throne room had killed her from the inside. She felt at fault and she admitted to all fairies, before she left, she had let them down and would go into the human world becoming a banished fairy.

Teatherwilly's seed ached that day as he watched his queen walk into the circular mushroom portal and cut her ties with the fairy world she had once ruled. He remembered watching her walk away in her human form, not looking back. He wanted to follow her, but he did not. He flew away from the portal to the southern part of the realm where the Darkness had not reached.

The Darkness had never reached the land where he lived. The darkness seemed to halt once she left. It couldn't be cured, but it didn't grow outward to the other trees either. It seemed Tygira had been correct and she claimed to be queen for saving the land. She promised every fairy that she would try to fix what had been damaged. This would be a promise she would not and could not keep.

Years later, the Darkness started its cruel way of consuming the woods, but it didn't spread as quickly as it had before. The Darkness seemed alive and Queen Tygira attempted to quell the Darkness with everything she had at her disposal. This, told to him by visiting fairies from Fairy Court. He no longer cared. His queen had been banished and she would not be returning.

As he flew, the scent of something sweet caused him to stop flying. He hovered, lifting his nose in the air to find the source of the strange aroma. "Sweet nectar," he proclaimed.

Looking down, he saw a long stick with something pink wrapped around it. The smell exuded from the pinkness. Did he have time to sample the sweetest smelling food his nose had the pleasure of ever smelling? He slowly flew down toward it, looking at Fairy Court in the distance. He figured it would only take a few bats of the wing to investigate this mystery food. He landed next to it, lifting his chin in the direction of the pink food as he took in a large breath of air through his nose. He shook from excitement, at the thought of trying something new.

Teatherwilly's mouth watered, his stomach growled.

"Only a little taste," he said to himself, holding his long fingers together as if pinching the air.

He licked his lips while looking around for other fairies that could see him. The second horns echoed through the morning air, making Teatherwilly jump. His hands fell into the wonderful pink food. He pulled them out immediately but became scared as the food came with his hands, sagging sluggishly toward the ground. Waving his hands seemed fruitless and even seemed to make it worse. The pink food started to crawl up his arms with his movement. His wings started to flutter as he lifted from the ground, pulling his body away from the danger he found himself entangled in.

Could this be the trap that has been whispered about throughout the land? If so, he now understood how dangerous it could be. His attempts at pulling himself away from the large blob of pink food tired him. He felt as if he were about to break free as his balance shifted from the elastic tendrils of the pink sludge. He fell from the air, his body becoming entangled in the strands of pink goo.

He stood from the ground and attempted to push the trap from his body, getting wrapped in it even further. He put a foot on the tree limb and attempted to push the trap away, but his foot slipped into the pink food. He started to panic and managed to immerse half of his body in the pink trap.

"Hello!" he yelled. "I seem to have gotten myself into trouble here."

No answer came from anyone.

The worst part of becoming stuck had been the loss of movement from his wings. He couldn't retract them. He stared longingly at Fairy Court. His voice would not be heard in court. The human children could be punished because he foolheartedly thought about his desire to taste new food.

"Help me!" he yelled, hoping someone would hear him and come to his rescue.

CHAPTER TEN
FAIRY COURT

Sam stared at the goliath tree in front of him as he kneeled cautiously behind a leaf that had been turned on its side. This tree, being hard to imagine, had been the very tree he and his family had tried to restore life to over the years. He wished he had known about the other force fighting against their attempts at saving it. Maybe his mother could have concocted a remedy for this…disease…plague…fungus. He didn't exactly know what to call it. He had no information on it, other than it being called the Darkness.

Now, that he paid closer attention to the tree, he noticed black veins webbing their way over the ridged bark, from the base toward the limbs, which lumbered over the land of fairies. He wondered if this *could be* a disease. He couldn't think of any disease that could cause plants to get black webbed veins. Of course, he stood in Fairydom. Anything could be possible now.

Taking his eyes away from the tree, he stood and started pacing in anticipation of seeing his children. Could it be that or had he been nervous about meeting the queen who had kidnapped his children? He knew his patience had started to run thin. He typically didn't anger, but in this situation, he felt very angry.

If the fairy queen refused to give his children back, he wondered what he would do to rescue them. He imagined running into the tree, scooping them up, and high-tailing it out before he could be caught. He knew that wouldn't work. There would be too many fairies against him.

It seemed like every option he thought of had the same conclusion. He could not just take them because he didn't know how to escape from here and return to his land. He knew he would need a fairy on his side who knew how to use the Fairy Ring to get them back. Flit would be that fairy, but he couldn't be sure if she would be held against her will if he rushed in for the rescue.

Sam rubbed his head in frustration, causing his hair to become messy. A large cluster of blackberries lay on the ground. Sam figured it must have fallen off a bush from somewhere high above.

Being this small, he now had to watch everything above him. He knew he could have been crushed by the weight of this berry if he had been under it when it fell. He had a new perspective as that of being a bug, and he didn't like it. New dangers were all around him and his children. He never thought he would have to worry about small berries falling from trees, hurting one of them.

A horn blew, causing him to duck to the ground on all fours. He crawled to the leaf and peered through a small tear. He felt adrenaline start to course through his body, giving him the shakes. A single fairy flew in his direction. She had the same wings of Flit, but they were spotted with color. The butterfly wings flapped in the air causing her to move quickly toward him. Could it be Flit? Did she see his children?

Flit landed on the other side of the leaf. "Your children are in there. The girl is sitting next to Queen Tygira."

Sam had mixed feelings now. He knew that Hillary would be having the time of her life. She sat next to a real-life fairy, a queen. "What about George?"

"He is…," she started to say and then paused.

"What?" Sam asked. "He is what?"

"The queen has him tied in a vine above Fairy Court," Flit said.

"Tied up?" George asked loudly. "I need to get in there."

"I understand," she said. "Let me make sure it is safe for you to walk to the Fairy Court."

"Flit!" a commanding voice yelled from behind the fairy.

Sam promptly lay down on the ground to hide from this unknown fairy while looking through the tear on the leaf. The view didn't seem that great, but he could see that Flit had turned around. Had he been seen?

A loud burst of applause came from inside Fairy Court.

"What are you doing out here?" the unseen fairy asked snidely.

"Asroth," Flit said, walking to him. "I figured you were standing with our queen."

"You didn't answer my question, Flit," he demanded, scanning the area behind her. His wings were nothing like Flit's. His were like dragonfly wings. Two pairs of translucent wings, two on top and two on the bottom, stood erect. The wings made an 'X' on the fairy's back. He did not retract them, which gave Sam the impression that this fairy didn't want to be caught off guard for any reason. "Why are you outside of Fairy Court? Who are you talking to?"

"No one," Flit responded. "I am talking to myself. I needed to gather my thoughts before I entered Fairy Court."

"Thoughts?" Asroth asked. "On what, might I ask?"

Flit seemed to hesitate and then answered, "The Darkness. I have been curious if I should ask for the status of a cure. I would like to aid in that endeavor if I could."

Asroth walked around Flit looking at the leaf keenly. "Why do you want to get your pretty little hands dirty with that nastiness? Why now? Do you have some type of information that could aid the queen?"

"No," Flit said stepping out of Asroth's way. "I just want to help. Since the Darkness is starting to spread faster, I could at least try to help. Queen Pasny has never asked for my help."

"And she will not ask," Asroth said. "You do have a certain…tie to it all, don't you?"

Flit remained silent as she looked at the ground, ashamed of his question.

"There wouldn't be anyone behind there would there?" Asroth asked.

Sam knew he had to do something fast or he could become a prisoner like his children and he wouldn't be able to help them. He turned his head to see if he could find some other type of concealment and spotted the cluster of large berries. He sighed, knowing what he needed to do.

****

Flit thought she had privacy out here. No fairy should have been out here. Everyone should be inside watching the queen make her way into the glamorous Fairy Court, everyone except Asroth.

"Now, Asroth," Flit said, pulling his arm back toward her. "Why would anyone be hiding behind the leaf? For what reason? You are becoming paranoid in your old age."

Asroth turned as she pulled his arms. He pointed his index finger at her. "I don't believe you are telling me the truth, Flit. I think you are hiding something from me."

"Fine, if you don't believe me, look for yourself," Flit said, looking straight ahead. "You will see there is no fairy in there."

Asroth looked at her sternly. "Queen Tygira requests for you to have dinner for her and her guests in her chambers."

"Very well," Flit said, slowly bowing her head. "How many guests will be attending, so I know how many berries to gather?"

"Two guests," he said, crossing his arms in front of him. Flit saw the cautious look in his eyes. Curiosity peaked in him. "The two will only require one berry."

"I will pick two berries for the queen," she answered. She waited for him to go. Asroth didn't budge. He stood in front of her, glaring. No. He stared behind her, at the leaf.

Asroth had always been keen. He is an elder of the land. Rumors spoke of his arrival to the land of fairies before the poison had been spread by the evil Pasny. He had been

168

granted leadership over the Queen's Royal Guard due to his loyalty to the fairies in the land.

"There are many who wish to topple Queen Tygira," Asroth said, narrowing his right eye as if he had felt pain. "I assure you, Flit, she will not be toppled."

Flit looked at him, perplexed. Why had he narrowed his eye and who would want to topple the queen? He seemed paranoid, more paranoid than normal. "If I heard of such a deadly act against our queen, I would have reported it to you. She is our queen. No other fairy could accomplish the things she has accomplished."

"Is that how you truly feel?" Asroth said, leaning toward her.

"Yes," Flit said. She didn't know why Asroth questioned her like this. Did he know she had brought a human into the realm?

"Good," he said, stiffening his body in a rigid military stance. "Our queen will be famished. I will see you in Fairy Court?"

"Yes," she said. She watched Asroth lift into the air.

Asroth did not fly back to Fairy Court as she expected. He turned away from the great tree and flew past Flit with determination. He flew to the leaf, to Sam's hiding spot. She would be exposed as a traitor. Why had she brought this human into their world? Would it be worth the price she would have to pay?

Asroth crashed through the dried leaf, leaving a ragged hole in the center. "What do we have here?"

Flit ran to the leaf, looking through the large hole he had made. She had already expected to see Asroth holding Sam. He hadn't been there. Asroth held a single black, shiny berry. The juice from the berry oozed slowly down the side of the berry and fell to the ground between Asroth's feet.

A cluster of blackberries lay on the ground on its side. Asroth seemed to have plucked one from the bundle. "I see you have already started your gathering."

"Yes," Flit said, resisting the urge to look around for her human companion. She watched as Asroth took a single bite out of the berry in his hands and tossed it to the side.

"Do you think the queen will be pleased with the berries?" Flit asked. She tried to sound excited.

"It is very good," Asroth said, wiping his hand on his pants. "I think she will be pleased."

Flit bowed her head. "Thank you."

Asroth walked close to her putting his face inches from hers. "Understand, Flit, I see you." He slowly walked around her. "I don't know what you are up to, but you will be caught. I don't trust you. The fairies that dwell in our land do not trust you. You bear the mark of Pasny."

"I am not Pasny," she said calmly, looking at the ground. She attempted to avoid the moldy smell coming from his breath. The smell seemed to surround her head in a cloud.

"Maybe not, but you are paying for what she did. All fairies that bear the mark will pay for what she unleashed on this land."

Asroth walked away from her and then took to the sky. The stench of his breath dissipated quickly. Flit let out a sigh of relief as Asroth flew to Fairy Court. He walked through the closed doors at the base of the tree.

"Sam," Flit said without raising her voice in alarm. She had been happy that he had not been caught but wondered where he could have gone. "Where are you?"

"I'm okay," a muffled voice said. The voice seemed to come from the large cluster of berries on the ground. Flit heard a 'humph' sound and the blackberry rolled over. Sam lay under it. Blackberry juice dripped from his clothes. He rolled over and got to all fours.

"I see you found a way to hide," Flit said, pointing to the bundle of berries.

"I guess," Sam said. He shook his hands wildly, trying to remove some of the berry juice. "I rolled one of the bundles over here and created a hole big enough for me to climb in. I wouldn't have imagined the smell being so strong. It's almost nauseating."

"I am sure there is some morning dew left in a leaf somewhere," Flit said, spreading her wings. She flew upward to a leaf and nodded her head. She yelled down to him, "Right here! You are going to have to stand under it, to wash the juice off your body."

Sam did as she said and walked under the leaf which hung off a bush, about forty feet above him. Flit tipped the leaf slowly and water flowed like a waterfall down to Sam, allowing

171

him to wash the majority of the juice from his body and clothes.

"Thank the fairies you weren't found," Flit said, flying down to him. She retracted her wings and hugged him.

"Luckily, the berry had fallen from a bush," he said, pointing up to the sky. "I kicked all of the clustered berries off the backside and slid into it. It's all I had at the time."

"Quick thinking," she said.

"I didn't want to get caught," he said, shaking his arms, attempting to get as much water off of him as possible. "Who came after me?"

"Asroth," she said. "He is Queen Tygira's advisor, a very cautious and paranoid fairy. He's always thinking that someone is trying to overthrow Queen Tygira. I don't know any fairy who would want to do that."

"If I had have been caught, the queen would have probably thought that," he said, looking at Fairy Court again. "What am I getting ready to walk into, Flit? He talked about a mark you have. Are you related to this Pasny?"

Flit lowered her head in embarrassment. "In a way, I am related to her, but only through Fairy Court. I have the wings of royalty like she did. Only the queen of fairies is born with the wings of the butterfly."

"So you're supposed to be the queen?" he said shocked. "Why aren't you?"

"It's a long story and right now we don't have time for me to tell it," she said, raising her head to him. She looked him in the eyes. "You have to trust me, Sam. You are not walking into anything bad. She has your children and we have the information she needs to help the fairies who were hurt by them."

Before Sam, stood a fairy claiming she should have been the queen because of her wings. He wondered if he had been talking to a crazy fairy. Were there such things as crazy fairies? He figured there had to be a few of them. Could he trust her because of her claim? He didn't have a choice.

"How do we get in there without being noticed?" Sam asked, looking at the tree.

"Let's go," she said. She flew to the tree faster than Sam could keep up.

Sam looked around the open area between him and Fairy court. He didn't see any fairies walking or flying around the area. He sprinted as fast as he could through the open, two-hundred yards between him and Fairy Court. He knew he had to be fast. There were no objects to take cover if a fairy were to suddenly appear.

He huffed and puffed during the run. He hadn't run in years and he could feel it. His legs started to ache and his lungs burned. He pushed himself hard and it paid off. He knew he didn't just run for his life, but the lives of his children.

The two-hundred-yard run ended with him at the doors of Fairy Court. He walked around in a circle trying to catch his breath from the jaunt. He felt his lungs expanding with air intake and collapsing as the air left his body. He had forgotten that he stood in the open once the blood started to flow back to his brain. He noticed Flit had disappeared.

He took in the beauty of the doors to Fairy Court. The casing of the double arched doors bore gold-encrusted vines. The doors seemed to be made of wood that had been sanded and stained with a bluish-green, glossy paint. Flowers had been carefully carved into the wood. Two golden handles, one on each door, were parallel to each other.

Sam grabbed the left handle and pulled it. Nothing. The door wouldn't budge. He pulled on the right handle. Nothing happened again. He pulled on both handles at one time and still nothing had happened. The doors were locked.

Sam shifted nervously, feeling very vulnerable. He looked around for Flit, even in the sky, but she had left him. *Where is that fairy?* Sam wondered.

He felt a hand grab his shoulder and pull him. Had he been caught? His arms went wild, grabbing at anything to gain traction from the pulling fairy. There had been nothing to grab. He watched as the sun suddenly vanished, leaving him in a cool, dim room. He noticed that the doors had not been opened. He seemed to have been pulled through them.

Inside the tree, he turned on the fairy that had pulled him in. He refused to go down this easy. He had his children to save and he knew nothing would get in his way. Flit stood behind him with her arms held up in a protective posture, holding a brown cloth. Sam relaxed, relieved that it had been her that had pulled him through the doors.

"Where were you?" Sam asked.

"Getting this," she said, holding up a cloak. It looked brown with swirls of black in it. The cloak seemed to be made from animal skin. "You will need to cover your ears and face."

"I didn't even hear the doors open," he said, taking the cloak. It felt heavier than it looked but wearable. He expected a stench to surround it, but only a sweet earthy smell came from it. He threw it over his body and pulled the hood over his head to hide his features.

"The doors never opened," she said, pointing at the closed doors. "I pulled you through it. It's a type of magical door, one that keeps unwanted creatures out of the tree. Only those of pure fairy blood can enter the internal parts of Fairy Court, or as I thought, be attached to a fairy while entering."

"This is never going to be easy," he said. He never believed in magic, but he did now. He didn't have a choice. All of this new fairy phenomenon had caused the wall he built between fantasy and reality to crash to the ground.

Sam looked around, inspecting his surroundings. Jagged crystals were stuck to the inside wall of the tree. They seemed to be placed randomly about. Did they grow on the walls? The dim light, allowing him to see, emanated from within these crystals.

Two shimmering curtains, covering the width of a doorway, hanged invitingly. They crossed each other, hiding what lay on the other side.

"Do we go through there?" Sam asked, pointing to the curtains.

"Yes," Flit said, pushing one of the curtains aside. She walked confidently into what Sam thought had to be the internal court where his children were being held. He followed, happy to know he would see them.

The view had to be the greatest spectacle he had ever seen. Fungus lined the crystal walls like stools. Fairies sat on the fungus waving their hands and cupping their mouths to either boo or cheer. The fungus flats, Sam named them in his head, circled to the top of the tree.

Many fairies were inside the court, some tall, some short, some didn't even look like they had faces. He saw mushrooms moving around in the lower part of the court. Some had stems of greenery growing from their heads like hair. He quickly realized this looked like an alien world. This scared him.

In the center of the court, a throne hovered in mid-air. A fairy, who Sam suspected is the queen, sat proudly upon the seat. She wore a silver gown that sparkled from unseen lights. She held a staff sternly in her left hand. Hillary sat beside the queen. He could see her moving across the throne looking at all the fairies around her. He suppressed the urge to wave at her. Where could George be?

"Queen Tygira," a tall, lanky fairy resembling a twig spoke. "Now that you have allowed the humans here, do you think Pasny will be able to return to our world?"

Asroth, the fairy who had almost caught him, flew from a large hole above the throne. He landed next to the queen and spoke close to her ear. She nodded her head. Sam swore a smile crossed her lips, a sinister smile. Asroth hovered next to her, crossing his arms. His wings were fluttering behind him creating a silver, rectangular blur.

"As your queen, I say you are in no danger," the queen announced, never moving from her proud position. "Pasny has been in the human world for far too long. She aged just as humans age. She is old and does not possess the power needed to do any more damage."

"But your highness," the same fairy interrupted her, "what if she does return to our realm? Would this be worth the risk of bringing the human children here?"

"I know she will return," the queen said. This caused the fairies in the court to gasp. She continued as if she heard nothing. "The human child named George only placed one trap. True, this creation is his doing, his responsibility. But I also believe that his creation has been placed throughout our land by one of the elderly human females."

"Then why have you brought them here?" a green-faced fairy asked. The green on her face looked like a tattoo of fire from her neck to her forehead.

"I have brought the humans here for one reason," she said, looking down at Hillary. "They know how to help the ones who are injured. They will tell us how to save them. I have the one called George in a vine trap above us. Once he helps, the children will go free.

"You fairies have the right to judge these humans," the queen said, lowering the staff, allowing the tip to quietly touch the base of the throne. "I would only like to see the humans help us repair what they almost destroyed."

Fairies talked amongst themselves.

Sam looked up into the hole and finally saw George, suspended above the throne, moving his feet. He seemed to be wrapped in a vine as Flit described. He became angry again. His son wiggled in a vine fifty feet above him.

"What will stop them from returning after they pass back into their world?" a yellow fairy asked.

"They find our land precious," the queen said. "They will not harm us. This I say as your queen. I have thought long and hard about bringing these humans into our world. I did it with a heavy heart, but I think these humans will help us heal the many fairies plagued by the sticky snare."

"Wait here, Sam," Flit said. "I am going to invoke a conversation with the queen. Everyone must hear my request."

"Hurry," Sam said still looking up to his son continuing to struggle against the vines. The feeling of helplessness felt dreadful.

Flit walked down a set of stairs toward some empty seats.

****

Queen Tygira touched Hillary's head and began stroking her hair gently. "I believe these children have been tricked by another human named Winstock. They have told me she is their nanny, a caregiver. I believe this Winstock is Pasny."

Hillary looked at Queen Tygira with a puzzled look. She felt confused by her statement. She wondered how Mrs.

Winstock could be called this Pasny who had brought so much devastation to the fairy world.

"Pardon me, your highness," Hillary interjected. She heard fairies below her gasp and saw many other fairies hold their hands to their mouth. Had she made a mistake by speaking to the queen? "Mrs. Winstock can't be Pasny."

Queen Tygira looked stunned for a few seconds and quickly composed herself. She stood from her seat and raised the staff again in her hand, waving it around. "Calm yourselves. She can understand and speak to us because I allowed her to. She and her brother need to hear what we are discussing."

The crowd calmed as requested. Every fairy looked at Hillary which made her nervous, but she needed to know why Mrs. Winstock had been blamed for something she didn't do.

"Child," the queen said, looking down at her with confusion crossing her face. "You don't have a word here. We will discuss this together in my chambers."

Hillary saw the queen's confusion and wanted to yell, but she did as the queen requested. She looked up at her brother. Her brother had stopped wiggling and looked back down at her with a big smile crossing his face.

"These children did not act on their own," the queen continued to address the fairies. "To be honest, my motivation in bringing the children here had been simply to get help with this sticky snare problem and show you there is much more going on here than two human children attempting to find us. Pasny will come here. She will be held accountable for what she has done. In banishing her so long ago, I thought the poison would go away with her departure, but I had been wrong. She will come and we will capture her. She will then help us rid our land of the poison and then be husked."

"Let the humans go," the yellow fairy said. "If they have the information to help our fellow fairies then I say let them help."

The vine holding George started to lower and bend to the throne. The vines started to unwind themselves from the boy's body. As the vine pulled back from him, George pushed against it angrily. It pulled away and went back into the hole above them. George stood safe on the throne beside Hillary. She hugged him and he hugged her.

"Are you okay?" Hillary asked.

"Yeah," George said, shivering as if he had seen a spider move across the floor.

****

Sam watched from below as the vine released George. He felt relieved once he realized that his children were safe. They didn't intend on imprisoning them as he thought.

Flit spread her butterfly wings wide and flapped them softly, allowing her to rise from the ground. Fairies gasped at this sight and moved back cowardly. "Thank you for releasing the humans, your highness."

Sam watched his children's faces light up at the sight of the colorful wings flapping. Queen Tygira's face snarled. She looked angry at this sight. Why had she looked so angry?

"Ah, Flit," the queen said. "I am so glad you are here with your now vibrant wings."

"I am happy to be here," she said, bowing her head.

"My fellow fairies," the queen raised her voice an octave above the tone she previously had. "Pasny will return and the fairy who flies before you will help her."

Flit looked up at the queen, bewildered. "Your highness, I only serve you as it has been mandated by the fairies of this land. I am bound to you and the welfare of this land."

"No, Flit," the queen said. "You are bound to this tree, like Pasny before you. You are not bound to me. You bare the same wings as Pasny and you pose a threat to the fairies that live here."

"I pose no threat!" Flit yelled, with a bit of force.

"Oh, but you do," the queen snarled, lifting her free hand into the air while spreading her fingers wide.

The ground below Flit started to rumble. Sam watched in horror as four vines exploded from the floor. They seemed to erupt from the ground so fast that parts of the tree were expelled into the air. Fairies that were near Flit backed away hurriedly, raising their arms to block the debris.

The vines nabbed each of Flit's appendages, confining her in mid-air. They seemed precise as if controlled by an unseen force. Flit batted her wings in an attempt to escape, but could not move. Sam started to run to her, to chastise the queen, but he had inadvertently been pushed into the wall by fleeing fairies. Chaos had broken out within Fairy Court.

Losing sight of Flit, he looked up to his children. The queen held her hand in a fist while smiling brightly. Asroth seemed perplexed as to why this could be happening. Hillary held a hand over her mouth. George took Hillary into his arms as if attempting to protect her from the chaos that had broken out below them. Sam found this comforting to know that his son would protect his little sister.

After the swarm of fearful fairies had flown out of Fairy Court, he finally had an opportunity to run to Flit. She struggled against the vines as they lowered her to the ground. He took one step and noticed the green vines started to turn black. Black streaks, like the ones he had seen outside of Fairy Court, started to appear on the vines. The streaks seemed to multiply as the vines started to break down. Decayed plant matter fell from the vines in chunks, freeing Flit. He watched Flit look down at her body as if she were confused as to how this could be happening.

"Do you see?" the queen yelled out in anguish to the remaining fairies. "She is poison. Flit is one with Pasny."

"I...I didn't," Flit said while turning to face the fairies, backed against their respected fungus flats. They seemed to cower at her pleading look.

Sam looked back up to his children. He wanted to yell at them. He wanted them to jump from the throne and join him so they could escape this madness. Would they too be wrapped in green vines, held captive by this tyrannical queen? Just as he decided to get his children's attention, he had been hit from the side and dragged out of Fairy Court. He reached out to his children, but it had been too late. The butterfly wings on Flit propelled them through the curtains and out of the tree.

Sam yelled at her to put him down. He yelled and she did not listen. His feet dangled in the air as Flit continued the blazing flight.

Just beyond the flatlands, between the large tree and the woods, Flit retracted her wings while they were still in the air. They rolled and then slid to a stop, feet apart from one another.

Before he could ask anything, Flit got to her knees and motioned for him to come to her with quick choppy waves of her hand.

"Hurry!" she yelled to him. "They will be coming for us."

Without question, Sam stood and ran to her. Surprisingly, he had not been hurt from the quick landing.

As he neared Flit, a grayish blob grew around them with a suddenness Sam had not expected. The light produced by the sun became dim, almost dark, once again. Had he been trapped by the queen? If so, he felt as if he were done with all of this. He needed to be with his children. They needed to feel safe.

CHAPTER ELEVEN
RELEASED

Asroth froze in astonishment as Flit spread her wings within Fairy Court, which had become colorful. Her wings had been white. Where had the color come from? Why had she done such a thing? Did she not know that Queen Tygira would see this as a threat to her within the walls of her sanctuary? He should have reacted, but the sheer notion of her actions stunned him. Everything happened so fast.

Memories of the past queen, Pasny, bubbled up from his memory.

He had witnessed Queen Pasny spread her wings one time in this manner. It started with a kiss on the hand and ended with one fairy losing his wings. Queen Pasny spread her wings once she recovered from the surprise that started the Darkness. Queen Pasny, Tygira, and the other woodland fairies barely escaped in the chaos.

He had frozen then as he did now. It seemed as if her vibrant wings produced a relaxant to those who watched her. He wondered if Queen Tygira felt the same effects.

By the time he became fully aware of the events taking place before him, Flit had flown through the tree. He had watched in awe as she flew into another cloaked fairy and pulled that fairy through the entrance to the court.

All fairy kind within the tree had scattered in all directions. Chaos had been created by Flit just as Queen Pasny caused chaos so many years ago. Asroth wanted to stop her before she escaped. He flew up into the throne room to gather the guards so he could stop another member of the Royal Tree Family.

****

Hillary had been amazed by the sight of the butterfly-winged fairy. According to stories told by Nana and Mrs. Winstock, this fairy should have been queen. George and she were told that one fairy so graceful and unique would be the leader of the fairies. This fairy possessed the colorful wings of a butterfly. They had both witnessed a fairy that fit this description, but she had not been the queen.

Instead of being queen, this fairy had been blamed for producing the very poison that killed the woodlands. Hillary witnessed this with her own eyes. Flit had blackened the vines and flew from Fairy Court. She wondered how such a beautiful fairy could be causing so much pain.

The children watched as Asroth, the crotchety old fairy in charge of the guard, fly upward to the throne room. Hillary knew that Asroth would find Flit and bring her back, just as he brought them here.

"Woodland fairies," Queen Tygira bellowed, looking around at the chaotic scattering of all the fairies. "She is gone. She is no longer a threat to us."

This did not seem to get the attention of any fairy. Hillary saw the irritation in the queen's face. Queen Tygira lifted her staff into the air and brought it down onto the floating throne with a crash. It sounded as if thunder had struck within the halls of Fairy Court. Hillary and George covered their ears from the sound. Queen Tygira's dragonfly-like wings shot from her back. They were not nearly as radiant as Flit's wings. They were almost underwhelming after seeing the butterfly-winged creature.

The loud echoing crack got everyone's attention. They all stopped and looked up to Queen Tygira.

The children removed their hands from their ears as the crackling ceased to echo within the wooden tree trunk. George put his arms around Hillary while standing behind her. They both looked down at the stunned faces of the crowd.

"Cease your movement," yelled Queen Tygira. "Flit is gone. She can no longer harm you. Her poisonous touch seemed to have stopped with the vines. She will be caught and punished for her blatant disrespect for your queen. As for these children, I do not believe they had anything to do with harming our kind. I mandate they be released to their land. They are now free."

Cheers erupted among the fairies below them. George started to feel much better about the situation they had found themselves in. He felt happy to hear that they would be returning home.

"We're free, George," Hillary said.

George wondered why she amended that they are returned without helping the injured fairies. Why would the queen bring them here, threaten them, and then want to send them home so fast? It seemed as if the queen had been unsure of her intentions.

"Please stay clear of Flit, my fellow fairies," Queen Tygira lectured. "If you have wondered why our land has not been healed, your answer lies in Flit's hands. She has betrayed us all and she will pay for what she has done."

Once again, the fairies below cheered for their queen as the throne began to rise. George and Hillary both sat quietly, taking in everything which had been seen and said.

"Mrs. Winstock can't be evil," Hillary said defiantly with a sharp tongue. She wanted to defend Mrs. Winstock. She wanted to make the queen understand that Mrs. Winstock could not be who she has been accused to be.

"You can't trust her, Hillary," the queen said rubbing her head. "This Mrs. Winstock is Pasny. I feel it."

The throne reached the throne room and stopped with a slight jar. George rose to his feet and took Hillary by her hand. He looked at her with the big brother's look. "Let's go."

"Where are you going, George?" the queen asked.

"Away from you," he said angrily, glaring at the queen. "You said we are free. Now I would like you to take us back to the ring so we can go home. When we leave, I'll bring back something that will help the injured fairies."

"George, you'll make her mad," Hillary said, turning to her brother.

"It is okay, Hillary," Queen Tygira said gently with a hurt voice. "George has every right to be angry. You were brought here on my orders. I feel as if I were wrong to do that, now that I know that your Mrs. Winstock is Pasny and that you had nothing to do with this. You may return home."

"Why did you threaten us?" George asked. "Why bring us here if you saw Mrs. Winstock place the gum around your land?

"I needed to make sure," Queen Tygira resigned.

George eyed her with caution. There appeared to be something else driving her that would bring them here and he didn't know what that could be. He quelled the anger and contempt he had for the queen. They were going home, which felt like the most important part of the deal.

"Would you please join me in my chambers for a drink, to celebrate your release?" Queen Tygira asked.

"Yes," Hillary immediately replied. George elbowed her, giving her a stern look, a look their dad would have likely given in these circumstances.

George wondered what this queen could be thinking. She had sent fairies to capture them. She then had him wrapped in a vine. Now she seemed happy and wanted to celebrate something which should have never happened in the first place. But a feeling of thirst overtook his desire to leave this place.

"Fine," George said.

"Please, follow me," Queen Tygira said, turning away from them. They walked down the empty corridor, following behind the queen. Her long dress moved elegantly as she strode to her chambers.

The corridor had become eerily empty.

"At one time this corridor had been white," Queen Tygira said, gently caressing the walls. "The darkness has turned it the color you see now."

The corridor looked nowhere near being close to the color white. The color looked dark-brown with streaks of black crisscrossing across the walls. George couldn't tell if the streaks were shadows or veins from the Darkness.

Queen Tygira stopped at two large wooden, double doors forming a large half oval. The polished wood gave them a wet look. She pushed against them slightly and they easily opened inward to a large obscure room saturated in an eerie green glow emanating from a chandelier in the center of the room.

Queen Tygira stepped through the doors causing the room to explode in crisp, white light, revealing lavish living quarters. Bookshelves filled with leaf-bound books lined the back wall. A large, fluffy bed that would beckon anyone to sleep in its grasp, lay just beyond the bookshelves. In the center of the room sat the shell of a snail laying on its side, creating a makeshift table. Four wooden stools had been neatly placed around the shell. On the right wall, a window had been covered in cloth.

Queen Tygira walked to the table and held her hand out, gesturing for the children to sit down. The two children didn't fuss about having to sit around a snail shell.

Queen Tygira released her gown which fell freely to the floor. She picked it up and hung it on a small peg protruding from the wall near the doors. Under the dress, she wore a purple dress that hugged her body tightly. She twisted her curly hair and wrapped it into a bun. She then removed what looked like a skinny stick from her arm and shoved it through the bun to make it stay in one place.

She sat down on one of the stools across from the children and steepled her fingers. "Now that we are away from prying ears, I can speak frankly with you. I need to know how you understood what we were saying in Fairy Court."

Hillary looked confused. George crossed his arms and felt confused by her comment. Hillary and George both asked, "What?"

"You could understand the conversation we were having in Fairy Court?" the queen asked.

"Yes," Hillary said.

"I could, too," George said. "What of it?"

"That is very interesting," the queen said as if deep in thought. "I never thought humans could be interesting. You are both human, therefore, you shouldn't be able to speak or understand our language."

"But you are talking like us," George said.

"No," the Queen corrected him. "I am speaking Fae."

"You told everyone you allowed us to understand you," Hillary said confused.

"I did, didn't I?" the Queen said. "Curious."

"You didn't do it, did you?" George asked.

"No," Queen Tygira said, taking in a deep breath of air. "It seems the realm is growing on you in a way I did not expect."

"What do you mean?" George asked.

"I don't know, George," the Queen said. "And that bothers me greatly. I am the Queen of the Woodland Fairies and I am at a loss for the answer."

"Okay," George said rudely. "If you can't explain that, can you explain why you think Mrs. Winstock is Pasny? She has been our nanny for years. She has taken very good care of us. Mrs. Winstock has been there for us when our mother vanished a year ago. She had been there when our Nana died last week. I refuse to believe that your Pasny is our Mrs. Winstock."

"Your Mrs. Winstock knows a lot about the fairies," Queen Tygira said calmly. George could tell by the queen's squinty eyes that she had become angry. "She taught Hillary how to bow to a queen. No human could possibly have known that. Only a fairy could know this. Not only did she teach her the bow, but she taught her the old way of bowing to a Royal Queen." Queen Tygira stood abruptly. She raised her voice. "That alone is proof enough for me to say that she is Pasny. That is proof enough for all of the fairies in this land to fear for their very lives. She has been trying to gain entrance to our land and I allowed the portal to be open because I never thought she would play two human children as fools. If she enters our land, she will continue where she left off."

She closed her eyes and took in a deep breath.

George and Hillary both looked at each other dumbfounded. Queen Tygira did not appear to act like any queen they had imagined. This queen looked nothing like what their Nana or Mrs. Winstock described. This queen strived on emotion and seemed very un-royal.

George stood. He could not comprehend everything Queen Tygira had said. Could his nanny, the very person who has cared for them, be this Pasny who had poisoned the land of fairies?

"Can you tell us about Pasny?" George asked. "Mrs. Winstock treated us well. She is like our second grandmother."

Queen Tygira walked to the curtain-covered window. She pulled it back, revealing a large circular window. After binding the curtain she placed her hands behind her back standing in a rigid posture.

"Pasny became infatuated with your kind. If she would not be here at Fairy Court, she would be at the border of our realm looking out to the humans. She would watch your kind with loving eyes. She never looked at me that way. She never looked at any fairy with that much love. I would watch her from within the woods. I saw her face light up every time a human would make an appearance from the white domain you live in now. She loved them. She cared for them. She loved them more than she loved us.

"She requested an audience with King Athgar, king of the Lawn Fairies. The Lawn Fairy domain is conveniently located right outside of your domain. I still think she wanted to meet with him as an excuse to get a closer look at the humans. Of course, the visit went horribly wrong. She kissed the top of King Athgar's hand as she always had. But this time proved to be a fatal kiss. The king collapsed to the floor as black veins stretched from the hand to the king's seed. Once his seed became infected, the rest of his body crumpled. That had been the first time the Darkness appeared. To this day, I do not know if King Athgar died from the kiss.

"A skirmish broke out between the two factions of fairies. One of the Woodland Fairies lost his wings. Queen Pasny had failed her people that day. She returned to Fairy Court and allowed the Darkness to seep into our land. For years, the Darkness claimed more and more fairy lives. At last, I could not stand it. I intervened, banishing her from our realm into the world she loved so much."

Hillary slid off of her chair in the middle of the queen's explanation. George waved his hand at her demanding that she get back to the table. He watched Hillary nervously while listening to Queen Tygira's account of Queen Pasny's demise.

George wanted to grab Hillary but didn't want the queen to notice her. So he walked over to the window to stand next to Queen Tygira. He felt a little more comfortable around her, but he still felt guarded. "Could the Darkness be accidentally made? It doesn't sound like Queen Pasny wanted to hurt anyone."

"It had been no accident," Queen Tygira whispered through her clenched teeth. "Many of the fairies concluded that it could have indeed been an accident. Because the Darkness had come from an unknown source and Pasny had been so loved by all the fairies she could only be banished. If I had my way, she would have been imprisoned in a seed husk which would have been buried deep within the ground."

George looked cautiously through the clear barrier that stood between him and the ground far below. The creek flowed through the woods far below them. Hillary pushed her way in between the two of them. George saw a look on her face he had seen hundreds of times. She had done something.

"Look, George," Hillary said, pointing through the barrier. "It's the ugly trees."

The plant that had grown on the other side of the creek had not been a tree at all. They had always called it a tree because the ugly plant didn't sound right. It had always been there and had never died. Small red flowers budded from it during the spring.

"Ah, yes," Queen Tygira sighed. "That is where three fairies are imprisoned."

"Imprisoned?" Hillary asked.

George saw Hillary look into the pocket of her pants and pat it gently. She had done something. She hid something in her pocket and he hoped Queen Tygira wouldn't find out about it. They had just got out of trouble and if Hillary had done something then they could find themselves in more.

"They were part of Pasny's guard who would not allow justice to be served," the queen said. A smile crossed her face. "I pulled their seeds and they turned into that mess."

"You killed them?" Hillary asked, horrified that a queen could be capable of doing such a thing.

"No," Queen Tygira said. "They are not dead. They are just not fairies right now. They are only a shell of what a fairy is. I guess you could call it hibernating."

"And you will pull the seed from the butterfly-winged fairy?" Hillary asked.

"Unfortunately, I cannot do that," the queen sighed. "My powers in this body only allow me to do so much. Flit, that is her name, is part of the Royal Tree Family. She had been born from the tree when Pasny left our land."

"So she should be queen?" George said.

"Yes," the queen said, turning to them. "But all of the fairies in the land agreed that Flit should never be the queen because she could have the Darkness in her and she might finish what Pasny could not accomplish."

Queen Tygira walked away from the window and went to a part of the room which might easily have been called a kitchen. "Let's forgo telling any more past stories. How about that drink I promised the two of you?"

A drink sounded good to George. That is the reason he agreed to come here, to begin with. Hillary continued to gaze through a clear barrier to the outside world. The height they were at didn't seem to bother her.

"What did you do?" George whispered to Hillary.

"Nothing," Hillary said, putting her hands in her pocket.

He knew she could not be telling the truth. Hillary had done something in here. "If you did something and the queen finds out, you will get in trouble and I am not going to help you out."

Hillary stuck her tongue out at George. This irritated him. He wanted to know what she had done, but arguing with her about it in front of the queen would not be smart. This would only bring unwanted attention to both of them.

"Here you are, children," Queen Tygira said while walking back to the window. She held a large goblet in each of her hands. The stem of the glass rested between her fingers while she cupped the bottom of the goblet with her palm.

George and Hillary both took the goblets. Hillary lifted the goblet to her lips. George stopped her with his free hand. "I'll try it first, Hillary. If it is good, I will let you have yours."

Hillary glared at George and drank from the Goblet anyway. "I'm not a baby."

George exhaled the frustration he felt and then gulped his goblet, tasting the sweetness of the liquid. There seemed to be something else hidden within the sweetness. The taste passed and the sweetness overtook his taste buds. He had a desire for more.

Queen Tygira clapped her hands together and smiled brightly as Hillary finished her goblet. "Did the taste meet your expectations?"

"It tasted sweet and fruity," Hillary said. "I want more."

"You can't have too much of a good thing now," Queen Tygira remarked. "That juice I gave you will have your thirst quenched for the rest of the day."

"When do we go home?" George asked.

"Soon," she answered. "I am waiting for Asroth to return. He is going to aid me in taking you home. But for the time being, I figured you would like to visit our world before you go."

"Yes," Hillary said excitedly. "I want to meet all of the fairies."

The queen laughed heartedly. "That would be impossible in just a few short hours, but I do have two fairies you can meet and they can give you the tour."

George got the impression that the queen had not told them the full truth. He felt as if Queen Tygira held them here for another purpose. He didn't know why he felt this way, it had been a feeling he got in the pit of his stomach.

Three knocks came from the door. "Ah," Queen Tygira said. "Here they are now. Come in."

Two fairies walked into the queen's chambers, one male and one female. They were both colorful. The male fairy had blonde, spikey hair, and the female had orange hair, split into three ponytails, one on each side of her head and one on the back of her head. When the two walked into the room, they stopped walking when they saw George and Hillary.

"Can it be true?" the female fairy said to her male companion. "Can it really be them?"

The male fairy stood next to the female with his mouth agape. It seemed as if he had met a movie star or a rock god.

"Hello," Hillary said, holding her hand out for one of them to shake her hand. Instead, both fairies stood perfectly still. Hillary thought she had done something to scare them.

"Say hello, you two," Queen Tygira said, urging the two of them to speak. "You wanted to meet the humans and now you have your chance."

Hillary dropped her hand.

"H-hello," the female said. "I'm Thily and this is-"

"Listle," he said quickly moving to Hillary. He turned her around and looked at her back and then pulled up her hair. Hillary snickered at this odd behavior. "You are human. I knew it."

Listle then went to George and repeated his odd way of meeting someone. George lifted his arms as Listle rotated around him.

Thily grabbed Listle and pulled him back. "Sorry. He is a bit rude."

"But they are human," Listle said. "Thily, they are real humans."

"Calm down, Listle," she said. She smiled apologetically at George and Hillary.

"George and Hillary will be staying with us for a little while," Queen Tygira said. "I am going to be placing the wellbeing of these two in your hands."

"Yes, your highness," Thily said.

"You can count on us," Listle said, snapping to a rigid stance.

"I will send word when we are ready to send them home," said the queen as she opened her wooden doors wide. "Now go and have fun."

The foursome exited the queen's chambers into the corridor. The large, wooden doors shut quietly behind them.

George started to get that weird feeling that the queen had lied to them, but he didn't know what secret she could be keeping. He didn't know how to find out either, so he let the feeling fade. Soon, he wouldn't have to worry about the queen or this land. Soon, Hillary and he would be home in the safety net of their house.

To be Continued…

Author's Notes

Thank you for taking the time to read what has become a large part of my life. When I first started to write this story I had no idea that it would turn into what it has grown to be. In the beginning, I wanted to put one novel together but later realized that it needed to be broken up into three books due to the length. In life, so much can happen in one day that can change a person's view of the world.

Now, be careful not to step on any insects. Maybe, just maybe, that little insect could be a fairy in disguise.

Made in the USA
Columbia, SC
18 June 2021